John Stark is a man with one purpose in life: to destroy the Company. Any way he can; regardless of who gets in his way. The Company is an international crime syndicate dealing in every kind of activity that will make money out of human degradation. It has killed everyone Stark holds dear and he is out to take his own kind of bloody vengeance on the murderers concerned. His path of revenge leads him from a prison break in England to the capital cities of the world, and behind him he leaves a trail of Company corpses. Stark is a hunter – hunted himself by his victims and the law alike.

John Stark is the Revenger.

Also by Joseph Hedges and available from Sphere Books

THE REVENGER: FUNERAL RITES
THE REVENGER: ARMS FOR OBLIVION
THE REVENGER: THE CHINESE COFFIN
THE REVENGER: THE GOLD-PLATED HEARSE
THE REVENGER: RAINBOW COLOURED SHROUD

The Revenger: Corpse on Ice

JOSEPH HEDGES

SPHERE BOOKS LIMITED
30/32 Gray's Inn Road, London WC1X 8JL

First published in Great Britain by
Sphere Books Ltd 1975

TRADE
MARK

Set in Times Roman

Printed in Great Britain by
Hazell Watson & Viney Ltd
Aylesbury, Bucks

ISBN 0 7221 4318 4

CHAPTER ONE

THE over-impressively named Ritz Hotel was not the best in the multi-island city of Stockholm, but it was pleasantly situated at the Karla pla end of Karlavagen. And it had a very pretty assistant manager named Inga Ohlson who lived in a two-roomed suite on the ground floor. Which was the reason John Stark was staying at the Ritz – rent free as far as money was concerned.

Stark had picked up the girl in the plush cocktail lounge of the Sheraton-Stockholm down on the Tegelbacken waterfront. She was young and new to her job, studying the methods of the Ritz's superior opposition. Stark told her he was an out-of-work post-graduate indulging himself in a little luxury after two weeks of seeing Scandinavia on the cheap. She was telling the truth. He lied. Even about his name, which he told her was John James. He lied smoothly and easily, in the same manner he committed greater sins and major crimes. But only when it was strictly necessary – to protect himself and to wage his constant one-man's-war against the forces of international crime.

'You're not John James at all, are you?' Inga said as the morning sun shone a bright yellow shaft through a gap in the drape curtains and spotlighted the top half of Stark's face. She spoke as his eyelids flickered in reaction to the sudden intrusion of brightness through the semi-darkness of the small bedroom.

Stark snapped open his eyes fully and smiled up into the face of the girl. She was much too young for her responsible job under-managering a seventy-five room hotel which with modernisation and a decent chef in the restaurant could make the first-class category. She was nineteen years old and an ash blonde with large green eyes, a pert nose and a small, well-shaped mouth. One day she would be beautiful and this promise was most apparent when, as now, she allowed her long naturally waved hair to hang as a richly-sheened frame about her face. When she was working she wore it in a severe bun.

But she wasn't working now. She was sitting up in bed, her back resting on a pillow stacked against the white laminated headboard of the double bed. And she was naked, her hands interlocked behind her slender thighs, hugging her legs against her small breasts. Her expression was pensive and a little hurt.

'Who am I?' he asked, holding the good-humoured look in place while his voice suggested a certain brittle hardness.

'You're John Stark. The Englishman the Stockholm newspapers call the Man Seeking Revenge.'

'The *Expressen* stole the label, darling,' Stark said, pushing off the continental quilt and swinging his feet to the carpeted floor. He was also naked. 'From the British papers. There just isn't a precise translation into Swedish of the Revenger.'

He padded across the room and through a doorway. Inga waited until the toilet had flushed and the shower started to hiss. Then she got out of bed and moved to stand in the open doorway. Her all-over tan told of her nude sun-bathing sessions on the hotel rooftop. The lush pubic triangle at the base of her flat stomach proved the natural coloration of her hair.

'The police do not know you are in Stockholm. How did you get here from Lakbörg?'

The village was on the shore of Vänern in the Swedish lake district, far to the south-west of the capital city. It had been the scene of Stark's last assault against the company. There, in a luxurious lakeside house, he had slaughtered three top executives of the Company's Scandinavian arm and a bunch of the organisation's enforcers.* The Scandinavian company was still reeling from the savage blow and the Swedish police were convinced Stark had escaped the country after the mass murder.

* See *The Revenger: Rainbow Coloured Shroud* (Sphere Books).

'In the back of an empty container truck as far as Örebro,' Stark shouted above the rush of needling water. 'Borrowed a car that ran out of petrol at Enköping. Then took a freight train into Stockholm.'

'You mean stole a car,' Inga said dully.

Stark shrugged and grinned through the teeming shower water. 'For a Swede you know your English semantics, darling,' he congratulated. 'All right, I stole a car. Maybe if I hadn't lost a bloody fortune when another car went off a bridge I'd have gone into the local Hertz agency and rented one.'

He stepped out from under the shower and started to towel his body and head. It was a powerful body, weighing a hundred and eighty-two pounds and standing almost six feet tall. The head was topped by thick, black hair which he wore long, but not overly so. The face beneath was a handsome one with clear blue eyes which were deep set, a well formed nose and a pleasant mouthline which smiled easily, above a slightly thrusting jawline. It was a lean face aged to about the right extent for a man in his late twenties; except that he had chosen to grow a bandito-type moustache which at first glance made him look at least five years older than he was.

He had entered the Sheraton-Stockholm with just ten American dollars in his pocket. His only luggage was a Luger Naval Parabellum P.08 stuck into the waistband of his trousers. Gin slings for Inga and himself in the hotel's cocktail lounge had used up most of what was left of the small fortune in company money, the bulk of which he had sacrificed to buy his survival on the silted bed of a water-filled quarry.

Thus, he used Inga's toothbrush and paste, Inga's deodorant and talc and then buzzed off most of his night's growth of beard with Inga's battery lady-shaver. Its blades were blunted after four day's of such misuse.

The girl watched him in sullen, pouting silence: and continued to survey him in the same manner when he moved back into the bedroom and started to dress. Her expression did not alter until he went to the built-in wardrobe and delved behind a pile of three suitcases to bring out the big German automatic. Then her green eyes registered shock and a gasp escaped her parted lips.

'I didn't know you had—'

Stark pushed the gun into his waistband. 'A gun didn't go with my image as a hiking student, darling,' he explained. 'I hid it. I'm crafty as well as a liar.'

'And a user of women!' she challenged. 'I've out-lived my usefulness and now you are going to leave.'

He saw moisture at the corners of her eyes and realised her peevishness was not simply on account of discovering who he was.

'Please?' she begged as he eyed her levelly. 'I'm sorry I told you I know. I don't care about what you've done. You don't have to go.'

It had been an easy, free-swinging relationship during the past four days; Stark confined to the small bedroom and only slightly larger living room. Alone during Inga's twelve-hour daily stint in her office and the hotel's public rooms. Then, together at nights, supplying the girl's near nymphomaniacal needs. An ideal arrangement for Stark, who had gone to ground in worse places when company and police pressure grew too hot in the open. And it was no hardship paying the price in kind to such a pretty, slim, firm-bodied landlady. Now was the first time he had realised the girl was getting anything except sex from the relationship.

'The last time this happened with a woman who wasn't a company fun-girl, she died the hard way,' Stark replied.*

'Because they knew who you were and where you were,' Inga argued. 'I made an educated guess, John. That old prison photograph in the newspapers doesn't look anything like you. It was just the way you'd never leave the room, even when it was safe. And how you were always behind the door when I came in. The police have been looking for an English fugitive, John. You've been acting like a fugitive and you are

* See *The Revenger: The Gold-Plated Hearse* (Sphere Books).

English. It simply occurred to me. And then, this morning while you were still asleep, I looked again at the picture of you in the newspaper. It seemed it could be you, much younger.'

'I haven't had a birthday since it was taken,' Stark replied. 'I used to look younger than my age. Killing's a vocation that puts years on a man.'

'That you are leaving . . . it makes me feel you do not trust me.' She moved towards him, eyes more liquid than ever, and arms held wide for an embrace.

Stark felt sorry for her. Not much, for since setting out on his campaign of revenge against the company, a great deal of his capacity for feeling normal human emotions had been wrung from him. But, looking at her, he knew that Inga loved him. Despite her slim nakedness and the expression of wanting on her pretty face, the trembling of her body against his was not triggered by lust. Inga just wanted to be near him and to have him stay with her.

'You told me you know,' he said, stroking her hair, gleaming as the shaft of sunlight caught it. 'If you'd just let me suspect, then maybe I wouldn't have trusted you. Okay, it was an impulse.'

She jerked her face out from his shoulder and tilted her head to look up at him. She smiled like a child just been promised a much-desired Christmas present. 'You'll stay?'

'The room's good and the service is terrific,' he told her, grinning. 'I'd be a mug to leave, wouldn't I?'

She was a head shorter than Stark and had to go up on tiptoe to brush her lips across his mouth. 'God, I'll be late for work!' she trilled happily as she caught sight of the bed-side alarm and saw the hands pointed to eight-fifteen.

Stark sat on the edge of the rumpled bed and listened to her shower, then watched her as she dressed. She had the exalted job of under-manager because she was the mistress of one of the board of directors of the combine which owned the Ritz. There was resentment towards her from some of the longer-serving members of the staff, but she took her job seriously. And she tried to overcome the animosity by being conscientious and good at it. When she was dressed in a modest and simple grey tunic and skirt worn over a white top, she kissed him again. More passionately.

'I know what you are really like, John Stark,' she proclaimed. Then she applied the light make-up which was all her natural youthful good looks required. 'Breakfast in five minutes,' she promised before pulling open the door and going out, stepping gaily, delightfully happy after the moments of depression.

Stark eyed the closed door impassively, having used up all the sympathy he could spare for Inga. The fact that, before the day was out, her new mood would be shattered was just hard luck. Apart from willingly and with great enjoyment supplying one of her basic needs as the female of the species he had done nothing to encourage her to get hung up on him. But, now that she had proved her deep attachment to him, he had to ditch her. And his motives had nothing to do with protecting her from the painful repercussions of her own emotions: or the lethal attentions of the company.

Four lonely days of missing Inga and five, by turns hectic and peacefully euphoric, nights of trying to isolate lust from something deeper, had showed Stark that he could easily become as involved with the girl as she was with him. So it was himself he was protecting with the decision to leave. He was engaged in a war where he had to be constantly prepared to think clearly and act fast at a split-second's notice of danger. A mind cluttered with sweet memories of a subtle perfume and a body aching for the next contact with a familiar curve of firm, warm flesh could not react at its peak capacity. And Stark might fail to survive because of this. But if he should live, there was the even worse stage of mental instability which the final parting, or even the grief, brought.

Thus, as Stark drew open the drape curtains, took off his jacket and waited for the gentle tap on the door, he was thinking solely of himself in planning his departure. Experience had taught him the hard way that it was the only consideration to take into account.

When the knuckles rapped against the door panel, he went out into the living room and crossed it with four long strides. He cracked open the door, pulled it wider and took the tray.

'I'll see you lunch time,' Inga whispered, and he closed the door without replying.

The tray held a coffee pot, cup and saucer, sweet rolls, butter and jam. Food was the only problem of living in Inga's cramped but comfortable quarters. But so far the girl had been able to provide him with three meals a day and not arouse suspicion. Breakfast and lunch came from the kitchen of the hotel's restaurant, she asking for a tray to be sent to her office, then bringing it to him. Evenings she got open sandwiches from a café on a corner across Karlavagen from the hotel. That was the only meal they had together. She had told him she skipped breakfast and ate a fast lunch in the same café each midday. Probably not enough, he decided idly as he ate the breakfast: she had been living on love.

The rolls and coffee finished, he moved from the low occasional table and stretched out in a deep armchair, setting his mind to work on a plan. He had not given a thought to leaving until this morning. Despite newspaper stories suggesting he had probably left Sweden, he had no doubt that the police and the company were still searching for him. The kind of heat he had generated, first in Denmark and then in this country, would take more than four days to go off the boil. But risks – calculated wherever possible – were as much a part of his vocation of revenge as killing. And, having made up his mind to leave, he was determined to do so.

Getting out of the hotel was no problem. Because Inga was on the staff rather than a guest, her rooms were situated at the unimpressive rear of the seven-storey hotel. Both bedroom and living room windows had a monotonous view across a patch of unmown lawn to a ten feet high brick wall. This was the back garden of what had once been a large private house on a side street leading into Karlavagen. But the house had long ago been converted to offices and none of the commercial tenants were inclined to maintain the garden. Thus was Stark able to move about both rooms all day in safety with no risk of being seen through the lace curtains hung at the windows. For nobody ever ventured out into the waist-high grass and weeds – perhaps because the bulk of the hotel kept the area in constant shadow. Under cover of darkness, it would be a piece of cake to leave through one of Inga's windows, cross the overgrown lawn, break in through the rear of the office building – deserted after the day's work was finished – and reach the side street via the main door.

Then he would have the whole of Stockholm before him. But he had no intention of remaining in the city – or in Sweden, even. Norway was the closest land frontier and there was also Finland, by land up through Lapland or the sea route across the Gulf of Bothnia. He knew the geography because he had filled his aimless days with books from Inga's extensive collection. Most of the volumes were erotica or outright pornography but there was also a world atlas and two guides to Stockholm in the living room bookcase. He discounted both Norway and Finland. Also Denmark to the south. For the Scandinavian arm of the company was an integrated one. The enforcers would be searching for him with equal keenness in every part of this northern chunk of Europe.

So it had to be a longer trip, which meant sea or air. He could reach Bromma Airport without running too many risks, but trying to stowaway on an outward-bound airliner . . . he shook his head to dismiss the crazy idea. It would have to be a ship, of which there would be no scarcity in a water-oriented place like Stockholm. And he would have to stowaway because he had no passport and no money to grease the venal palm of a ship's officer prepared to by-pass documentation for other considerations.

'It's going to be dodgy, mate,' he hissed to himself. 'But when a bird on the nest wants more than a lay . . .'

He allowed the soft-spoken sentence to trail away, then grinned to swamp his regret. He rose from the chair, slid the two guide books from the shelf and returned. For the next three hours he studied the street plans of the city, ensuring that he was fully familiar with the layout of Stockholm, spread across the more than twenty bridge-linked islands. He paid particular attention to the dockland area but he also studied the city as a whole, noting how to reach his objective from every point: on foot, by (stolen?) car, bus, underground railway and water – swimming or in a small boat. Whenever his eyes lighted on the arrowed sign pointing west along Drottningholmsvagen towards the airport he experienced a stab of disappointment. When he moved, he liked to do it fast – sometimes because his life depended upon it and often simply because he enjoyed speed for its own sake.

Once, he even rose from the chair and made a thorough search of the rooms. But there was no cash around. The nearest he got to money was a bank statement showing Inga had amassed savings of a thousand *Krone*. About a hundred pounds sterling. She didn't even have a passport he might have been able to doctor.

The girl brought him lunch a little after midday. In the brief period while the door was opened to pass in the tray, he saw the look of sadness marring her pretty face.

'I'm sorry,' she muttered and for a moment Stark thought her feminine intuition had warned her of his intention to leave.

Then he saw the folded sheet of hotel letter-heading on the tray. The message was short and hurriedly written:

John – The monster telephoned. He wants me to have dinner with him tonight. It will mean going to Östermalm. Please stay, darling. Inga.

The monster was the girl's meal ticket who was rich enough to have a house on the upper-crust island of Östermalm and indulge himself with more than one sexy young girl friend. This was the first time since Stark had moved in with Inga that the lecherous old man had demanded another bite of the cherry for which he was paying so highly.

Stark ate the beef salad with relish, taking a more amenable view of the horny old stuffed-shirt than the girl's word pictures of him had presented previously. For with Inga engaged elsewhere there would be no tearful farewells to clutter his clean break from the Ritz.

He slept away the afternoon and woke in time to shower and shave again before Inga knocked on the door and he let her in shortly after eight-thirty. She had the usual paper bag of open sandwiches and he ate them while she rushed about between the bedroom and bathroom, showering, donning evening clothes and then making up her face for the date. She did most of the talking and her chatter became lighter as Stark's responses maintained a high level of good humour. She went out of the door at nine, entirely convinced he would still be there when she returned.

Full night swooped down to do battle with the lights of Stockholm at ten-thirty. Stark had the Luger held against his hip by the waistband of his trousers and was shrugging into his jacket when knuckles tapped on the door. He cursed under his breath. The lights in both rooms were already out in preparation for him slipping out through the bedroom window, invitingly open. He considered making a fast exit, but at once dismissed the idea. Inga had a key, of course: knocked only because he insisted upon it, using a made-up morse code signal cadence. If he didn't open the door, she would use the key. He knew about the woman-scorned syndrome. A nymphomaniac scorned was likely to be even more of a wildcat and it would take him time to get into, through and out of the office building.

As he cracked open the door he realised he hadn't listened to the knock carefully enough to be certain it had the right number of raps correctly spaced. Familiarity breeds contempt, he mused with a soft sigh as he looked at the girl standing in the passageway outside. A girl as tall as he was, with red hair cropped short and hugging her head. A girl with a cute face and dark eyes. A girl of twenty-five or so with a voluptuous body. The wrong girl – and close to being a dead one as Stark's free hand curled around the butt of the automatic.

'Hi, feller,' she greeted, flashing a toothy smile full of western promise. Her voice was a transatlantic drawl. 'Inga sent me to keep you from getting lonely. My name's Belinda.'

In Copenhagen the company had assigned its entire complement of fun-girls to a search and destroy mission aimed at Stark. Belinda had all the necessary equipment to work for the company's vice ring. But then so did every female in the world between twelve and thirty-five who didn't have warts on her nose. This one had freckles on hers.

'Tell Inga I'm curled up with *Lady Chatterley's Lover*,' Stark said, and started to close the door.

Incredibly, Belinda showed even more beautiful teeth when she broadened her smile. But there was nothing garish about all that white enamel. Her big dark eyes kept everything in attractive perspective.

'He was a male gamekeeper, and a fag you're not, Mr. Stark.'

'The lousy bitch!' he rasped, dragged the door wide, shot out an arm, clawed a hand at the front of her dress and jerked her into the room.

The smile was wiped away and a choked cry escaped her suddenly compressed lips. When he released her, momentum sent her staggering across the room. Stark closed the door softly. The front of the girl's knees hit the arm of the easy chair and she sprawled across it. Her dress was short length and snug fitting. When she rolled to the carpet the hem was hiked up and a lot of sensuously tapered thigh was exposed. Ample light dripped from the upper floors of the hotel to filter through the lace curtains at the window. Enough for Stark to see Belinda as she struggled angrily to her feet and for her to see him – to see especially the Luger he was pointing at her.

'Jesus Christ Almighty!' she gasped. 'Is that any way to treat a lady?'

'Ladies don't come knocking on the doors of strange men at night dressed the way you are,' he replied. 'That establishes what you ain't, darling. Now tell me what you are?'

She was smoothing her dress, head down so he couldn't see her face. When she did look up, her freckled features wore a hang-dog expression. 'A friend of Inga's. I work in the restaurant upstairs. Cashier. I'm between men right now. Inga knows it. She called me. I have an apartment not far from here. On Linnegatan. She said you and her were supposed to make it tonight. But she had a date she couldn't break. With Luthman, I guess. She didn't say. She said to come over to keep you company.' Belinda did some more dress-smoothing, this time concentrating on the bodice where his fist had bunched and creased the material. It was excitingly coned by her breasts. Her hands smoothed the fabric over the swells with careless sensuality. 'I'm sorry,' she said, looking up. 'I'm not a very subtle person.'

'Especially in the way you toss words around,' Stark agreed. 'Is that what she really said? That you were to come around and keep me *company*?'

She didn't react to the verbal stress. She simply looked confused. Then she replaced the expression with anger. 'Sure. What she didn't say was that you were a bloody sadist.' She advanced towards him, then veered to the side. She had to go around him to reach to door. 'I was ready to do Inga a favour. But there are limits to friendship.'

Stark held out his gun hand, the Luger pointing away from her. But his arm presented a bar against her thrusting breasts. She halted, and swung her head to meet his gaze on a level. He became aware of her perfume. It held that blend of strong-gentleness that advertised a high price tag. Anger continued to show in her dark eyes, but it looked ready to melt into something else.

'Limits are set to be stretched, darling,' he said, cracking his mouth to exhibit a grin that didn't reach his eyes.

'Meaning what?' she pouted.

'Meaning peel off the clothes so I can see how you stack up as a friend.'

She back-tracked, and a trace of a smile decorated her lips without revealing all those teeth. 'You do a fast turnabout, feller. And you don't waste much time in other directions, either.'

'We're just two very unsubtle people,' he replied.

The dress had button fastenings down the back. She had to contort her body with exciting effect to reach them. Her hands went first over her shoulders, then dived under her armpits. But Stark didn't watch. He left her to strip in the centre of the room while he went to the window. He opened it and checked the overgrown area, then raked his eyes up the rear face of the hotel. Belinda was down to a black bra, half slip and whatever she wore under that when Stark closed and latched the window and moved into the bedroom. In there he closed and latched another window, temporarily blocking his escape exit. Back in the living room he realised he had forgotten about the girl's shoes. She was now naked except for these, the high heels helping to shape the curves of her long legs. He treated her to the briefest glance before trying the door to make sure she hadn't put it on the catch. Then he turned, leaned against the door and surveyed her.

She did her sun-bathing with more inhibition than Inga. Her tan was darker, but her body was striped with the white images of a bikini across her breasts and lower belly. The large rings of nipples and the broadly based inverted triangle of her sex beard relieved the virgin paleness of breasts and belly. No, virgin was the wrong word to apply to anything about this girl, Stark thought. The way she posed provocatively for him, exhibiting every facet of her nudity without embarrassment told of a lot of experience flowing through her breech since it was first broken.

'You like what you see, feller?' she asked breezily.

Her large breasts sagged a little sans the bra and her stomach muscles were out of condition. But it was a good body with a lot of latent strength in the wide hips and incredibly long legs.

'There are a lot of ways of carrying your load, darling,' he answered. 'Somebody did a good job on you.'

'My maker and my dietician. Are you just going to talk about it or what?'

'What.'

She was confused. 'I'm sorry?'

'Living rooms are for living.' He waved the gun towards the bedroom door, then thrust the Luger into his pocket.

The smile without the teeth again, then she pivoted and wobbled into the bedroom. The heels of her shoes were ridiculously high, but there was nothing funny about the swaying action they caused in her rear end when she walked.

'And bedrooms are for bedding,' she said throatily. She kicked off the shoes. The bed was still rumpled from last night. Belinda overcame this with ease. She simply swept the padded quilt to the floor. Then she arranged the two pillows in the centre of the bed and draped herself over them. The hump arched her back, thrusting her belly upwards in blatant readiness.

'It's a recorded fact that most people die in bed,' Stark told her coldly.

Her head snapped up, to peer at him with terror-filled eyes. But his long strides took him to the side of the bed before she had a chance to do more than this. Her tanned thighs were already parted. Their firm flesh trembled and she sucked in the bulge of her belly as contact was made. The thighs came together, trapping his hand. It was fisted around the Luger butt, his index finger curled in front of the trigger. An inch of the cold barrel was sunk inside her.

'Jesus Christ Almighty!' she gasped, her hands clawing at the sides of the mattress.

'You came here for some action,' he told her softly, and used his free hand to jack a bullet in the automatic's breech. 'And I'm about ready to shoot my load.'

CHAPTER TWO

TERROR held the girl rigid on the bed. For a few moments she could not even move the tightness out of her throat to suck in air. When she did, her vocal chords were still affected.

'Please, don't!' The words were whispered and harsh-sounding.

'You've almost got the right tone, Belinda,' Stark muttered. 'Keep it low but feed in a little more passion. And add a few moans every now and then.'

Her large eyes grew wider and became locked by his cold, low-lidded stare.

'Do it!' he hissed and twisted his wrist back and forth in the warm firmness between her clenched thighs.

The foresight of the Luger snagged on the girl's clitoris and she flung her head back on to the bed and vented a low scream.

'Terrific,' Stark rasped, then abruptly became aware that it was not his order to which the girl was responding.

When the scream ended, she began to moan and her lips formed pleading words which did not emerge. Her belly rose and fell and then rotated. Her thighs parted to open the trap on his hand: but not to release him. She bore down against the pressure of the gun, gaping her sex to suck the ungiving metal of its barrel deeper inside her.

'Yes ... yes ... yeeeesssss!' she forced out between clenched teeth bared by curled-back lips. 'Oh ... oh ... oh ... Please ... yes ... yes ... please ... Sweet Jesus Christ Almighty. What am I doing?'

One of her legs was blocked by Stark's hip as he sat on the bed. The other one draped over the far side of the bed. Sweat sheened her naked flesh which writhed more frenetically as her lust drove her to try to take the entire length of the gun barrel inside her.

Stark stared in fascination at the demanding body and

passion-contorted face of the girl on the bed. For vital seconds the vivid tableau of such a high degree of sexual want going to waste aroused him: blotting out of his mind the object of the action which had sparked Belinda's frenzy.

'Please don't hurt Miss Jarratt, Mr. Stark.'

He had missed the opening of the door; its closing; the gliding of the man across the living room: and he had no idea how long the man had been framed in the bedroom doorway. But the soft-spoken words swept the lust from his mind. And Belinda became like a statue. Rigid, cold and unfulfilled. Then, as Stark swung his head to look at the man, the girl's frustration rasped out of her in a sigh that sounded like a dying breath.

'Miss Jarratt's feeling no pain at all,' Stark said. 'But if you don't drop the gun, mate, I'll blow out her brains.'

He knew the girl's name and he knew she wasn't too fussy how she got her sexual kicks. He knew the man had the same transatlantic background as she did. That was all he knew about either of them, except that they were not company. If they were, he would be dead by now. Maybe Belinda, too, sacrificed to achieve the objective of taking out The Revenger. But the gun Stark had ordered to be ditched was hanging loosely from the man's hand, on a level with the top of his thigh and pointed at the carpet. He released it without hesitation. On the floor it looked even smaller – a three-inch barrel hammerless Smith and Wesson ·32 revolver.

'I've been a complete and utter fool.'

He didn't look like one. He was a big man with broad shoulders and a thick-set neck supporting a dignified-looking head. Below iron-grey hair, short-cropped, he had a high forehead, neat eyebrows, clear grey eyes, hawkish nose and a thin, well-shaped mouth. He looked intelligent and rich, his expensive grey suit with the sheen of high price rather than long wear. He was about fifty from his skin texture, but he carried his years well.

'If that was a crime who'd be left to guard the prisoners?'

Stark asked, and eased the gun muzzle from its soft, moist resting place.

'May I get dressed, Mr. Groves?' Belinda asked. Her tone was incongruous: she spoke in the manner of a secretary asking the boss if she could take an early lunch break.

'I feel Mr. Stark is in charge here, my dear.' He had a deep voice and his tone was melancholy.

'Mr. Stark?'

Stark stood up, caught hold of a corner of the quilt and lifted it on to the bed. He draped it over the girl's nudity. 'You're decent enough for now. Draw the curtains and switch on the light Groves.'

The man complied. He was a natural glider, his footfalls hardly making a sound as he crossed and recrossed the room. The sadness in his eyes was even more apparent in the soft glow from the bedroom's two floor lamps.

'Okay,' Stark said, still holding the Luger but pointing it at nothing in particular as he leaned against the bathroom door jamb. 'The newspapers have written all there is to know about me. You decided to test whether I really am a sucker for a good looking bird. I am and it could have got me killed. But I'm still alive – and I'm liable to start kicking if you don't have a good explanation for this crazy charade.'

'Tell him what you know, Miss Jarratt,' Groves invited, and sank wearily into a wicker chair to one side of the door. In the higher level of lighting he looked sadder and older. Probably because of dark shadows under his eyes and the unhealthy pallor of his skin which were just two side effects of a lot of sleepless nights.

The freckle-faced Belinda spoke evenly and clearly. She was almost unrecognisable as the girl who had indulged in the mild orgy with the Luger barrel a few moments earlier. 'Mr. Groves has been looking for you for several weeks, Mr. Stark. Ever since he first read about you in the Toronto newspapers after your exploits in France.* He brought me to Europe to help find you.'

* See *The Revenger: Arms For Oblivion* (Sphere Books).

'You've found me. Maybe that could be wonderful for all concerned in the long run. Right now it scares me into having an itchy trigger finger.'

'We had a stroke of luck,' the girl replied, wriggling her body to sit up against the headboard, careful to keep herself covered with the quilt. 'The police or the people who want to kill you could have had it, but it so happened it was us. We were still in Copenhagen when we heard the news of what happened at Lakbörg. As you said, the newspapers have printed a great deal about you. Apart from your fondness for women, you are also known to prefer cities to the country. Sweden has many large metropolitan areas, but Mr. Groves decided to make our headquarters Stockholm. He intended to hire private detectives to cover other cities. He did that previously in other countries.'

'You don't look like a gambler, Mr. Groves,' Stark put in.

'A desperate man is prepared to clutch at any straw.' And desperation showed in every plane of his face; and in the slumped posture of his powerful frame.

'In this case, it didn't prove necessary,' Belinda continued. 'Our stroke of luck was that we checked into the Sheraton-Stockholm Hotel.'

'I don't remember posing for any pictures for the Canadian papers,' Stark interrupted.

Again, it was Groves who supplied the answer to Stark's query. 'An English-speaking man who looked even vaguely like those fuzzy newspaper half-tones was a straw worth clutching.'

'I followed you and the girl to this hotel,' Belinda took up her story again. 'I told the truth about working in the restaurant upstairs. And Mr. Groves rented an office in the building across the back area.'

Stark was getting angrier by the moment. A cold anger, held inside and directed at himself. He had been in Inga's rooms for almost a week now. And the whole time he had been under surveillance without knowing anything about it. Only luck had decided it should be this ill-matched couple of screwballs rather than company enforcers who had pinned him down.

'We knew after a couple of days that you had to be John Stark.'

'So why did you wait so long to pull this crazy stunt?' he wanted to know.

'Crazy maybe, but it worked,' Belinda answered quickly, showing emotion now. Her voice and the big eyes challenged him to argue the point. Then the spirit drained out of her. 'Though not the way we anticipated. Inga and I became quite good friends over the past few days. It was she who hired me for the job. She never mentioned you, but she did talk about Luthman. She told me he was taking her out tonight. I got a passkey from the cleaners' room and gave it to Mr. Groves. Then I came here to keep you distracted so he could make this approach. It wasn't meant to be so . . . so . . . unnatural.'

'Between consenting adults, anything goes,' Stark said, then swung his attention to Groves. 'Why didn't you try just knocking on the door without a gun in your hand, mate?'

'Because I am a complete and utter fool,' he re-iterated. 'And a coward, too, no doubt. You have been on the run for a long time, Mr. Stark. I thought you might be inclined to react violently to any direct approach. I abhor violence.'

'The gun was just to give your jacket a better drape?' Stark said wryly.

Groves poked at the revolver with the pointed toe of one of his high-priced leather shoes. 'A further indictment of my crass stupidity. To defend Miss Jarratt and myself until such time as we could convince you we meant you no harm.'

The fire of self-directed rage still glowed in Stark's belly, but with less ferocity. Groves spoke, looked and acted like a normally intelligent man motivated by anxiety into behaving like a reckless fool. Belinda Jarratt also was not a mindless imbecile. She had something for the man and it was no hardship for her to indulge her appetite for sex to help him. Crazy as it was, their story rang true. In which case he had to believe that luck had led them to him – and be grateful that fate had smiled on them rather than the police or company.

'What do you mean for me?'

'A way out of your immediate difficulties,' Groves replied. 'It wasn't simply for the right opportunity that I waited so long to approach you after assuring myself you were the right man. I knew it wouldn't be easy to convince you to trust me. So I spent some time amassing material proof of my good intentions. In the office I rented is a British passport with description details which match you. It requires the addition of only your photograph and any name you choose to use. There is also an open Air Canada ticket from Stockholm to Toronto, one-way. Some luggage ready packed with clothes I am certain will fit you. And traveller's cheques issued by a London bank to the amount of one thousand pounds sterling. Unsigned, of course.'

Groves had said he was rich and it was obviously no lie. Having gone to the expense of tracking Stark all over Europe the cost of getting together the material he listed would have been negligible – even the illegal items.

'What do you plan to buy with all that?' Stark asked.

'You're an expert in certain fields and I think you have some time to spare. I wish to purchase your time and your expertise, Mr. Stark.'

'To do what?'

'Miss Jarratt is a loyal employee whom I trust implicitly. She knows there is just one reason why I will not discuss that matter in her presence. I will not have her involved.'

In a short pause the silence was heavy and tense. The bedside alarm ticked disproportionately loud. It reminded Stark that a lot of time had passed since Inga went out for the date she knew she wouldn't enjoy. She wouldn't allow it to last any longer than necessary.

'Where's the office?'

'Second floor front. The door at the head of the stairway. The sign says Svensk Manufakturisten.' He sat more erect in the wicker chair and there was more life in his tone.

'Get your clothes on, darling. And go with him. If I don't come calling in half an hour you're the only one who got anything out of this mess.'

The girl slid off the bed hurriedly, but not carelessly. The quilt stayed firmly wrapped around her until she went from sight into the living room.

'This is totally on the level,' Groves assured while Belinda dressed. 'I would have brought the papers but . . . if there was trouble.' He became shame-faced. 'I couldn't stand any scandal.'

'We all have our hang-ups, mate,' Stark told him acidly. 'I have this thing about people who try to get to me on the sly. Especially people with guns.'

'Keep it.'

'I intend to.'

They remained silent until the girl re-appeared, looking sexier then ever in the snug dress now that Stark knew what it concealed. She found her shoes and put them on.

'Okay, go and start the night shift at the office,' he told the couple.

'I'm relying on you, Mr. Stark,' Groves said as he and the girl reached the door to the passageway. 'I swear that everything Miss Jarratt and I have said is the truth.'

'I'm almost sold,' Stark answered, picking up the small revolver. 'I just have to be sure it's not up the river.'

He waved both guns at them and they went out. The moment the door was closed, he pressed the switch to turn out the bedroom lights. Then, pocketing the smaller gun, he went to the window, opened it and checked the area. Twenty company enforcers could have been hiding in the long grass: twice as many more at the darkened windows of the office building.

'Think positively, mate,' he rasped to himself as he swung a leg over the sill and slid out of the window.

Somebody was playing a radio or record on a higher floor of the hotel. The male voice sang sweet and low. It provided enough noise to cover the small sounds Stark made angling through the overgrown lawn. Some crumbling concrete steps led up on to an uneven patio. The singer reached for a high note and his voice cracked. So did one of the small panes of glass in the door from the patio to the office building. The sound of the Luger barrel smashing the window was shockingly loud. The broken shards dropping on to some kind of cushioned floor covering was a pleasant contrast. The door was fitted with a Yale lock or the Scandinavian equivalent. It had not been used in a long time. It groaned in protest but turned. The door hinges squeaked in a minor key. Stark glided through, re-closed the door and peered through the hole in the pane. Nobody was looking down from the illuminated windows at the back of the hotel. Darkness blinded many others but Stark did not waste time searching for suspicious shadows. He was in a room that smelled of furniture polish and stale dirt. A door at the side gave on to a broad passageway running through the building from front to rear. The stairs canted up on the right a couple of yards from the front door. Stained windows flanking the door allowed in enough street lighting for him to see where he was going.

Each flight of stairs was dark but the landings had pebble-glass windows which gathered in more street lighting. The door which faced him when he reached the top of the second flight of carpeted steps was lettered with a whole list of multi-syllable Swedish names. None of them said Svensk Manufakturisten. Then he realised the reason. On first impression he had taken Groves and Belinda for Americans. But they had talked about Toronto and Air Canada. So maybe they came from north of the forty-ninth parallel. And maybe Canadians numbered their building storeys the same as Americans, missing out the ground floor. So he went back down a flight and found the marked door as specified by Groves. A sign on the wall said it was the mezzanine floor. The door was locked, of course. So he waited in the shadow of a doorway further along the landing.

Not for long. The side street was a quiet one at this time

of night. He heard the clicking of Belinda's high heels on the pavement. Loud enough to cover the sounds of Groves' progress. Up some concrete steps. Then a key rattled in a lock. The door opened and closed and the couple mounted the stairs. Stark waited until Groves had opened the office door before he stepped forward.

The girl gave a gasp of fear. Groves' face was suddenly pale in the meagre lighting.

'Sorry,' Stark said without meaning it. 'And I hurried to get here fast to save you worrying about me.'

He had the Luger in his hand still and he used it to wave them both inside. Belinda hurried across the room to let down and close some venetian blinds. Groves switched on a flexible-armed desk lamp. Svensk Manufakturisten had not left much behind. Just a rickety desk and a swivel chair, the lamp and a telephone. Paler patches on the smoke-darkened walls showed where other furniture had once stood against them and pictures had been hung.

'We are naturally nervous,' Groves excused as he dropped into the chair and used a tiny key to open a desk drawer. 'In making an approach to you we are laying ourselves open to the interest of the police and the company.'

'It was a risk you chose,' Stark pointed out, moving across to the desk to look at the passport, airline ticket and pad of traveller's cheques which Groves took from the drawer and fanned out over the scarred wood. Over the edge of the desk, standing beside the chair, he saw two pieces of matched luggage. The finish looked like real leather. He kept hold of the gun and examined the stuff on the desk more closely. He saw that the passport listed its owner's occupation as a travelling salesman. He nodded.

'Leave us, Miss Jarratt,' Groves said.

She went out of the office like an obedient dog. She closed the door and they heard her retreating footfalls, muffled by the carpet on the stairs.

'I want you to kill a man.' He said it in the tone of a boss finally telling his secretary it was all right to go to lunch.

'A man who keeps a particular kind of company?'

'Precisely. If it were not so, I could have got myself an assassin with much less effort and expense.'

'In Toronto?'

'In Canada. Somewhere.'

'It's a big country and I've never been there. You can narrow it down?'

'Somewhat.' He shot his cuff and looked at the dial of a watch held to his wrist by a gold band. 'I intend to be aboard the one o'clock flight to Montreal. There's a three a.m. departure for Toronto through New York. You will be met at the airport by a car. We will meet and I will give you the full details of what I require you to do. Security is strict at Canadian airports. Probably here in Europe, too. You should not risk taking the guns. I will be able to supply you with weapons in Canada. Indeed, I will be able to give you anything and everything you need to complete this assignment. Are you prepared to take the flight on these terms?'

Stark pursed his lips. 'You've spent a lot of money finding me and putting together the stuff to get me to Canada, Mr. Groves. The thousand pounds is—'

'A down payment,' he cut in. 'I will, of course, cover all expenses. And, after you have finished the job, I'll give you ten thousand dollars in any currency you choose and arrange for you to stay safely in Canada or assist you to leave.'

Again the Luger had been pointing at nothing in particular since he entered the office. Now he thrust it into his pocket and extended his hand. Groves' grip was short, weak and clammy.

'It's a deal.'

Groves opened a drawer that had not been locked. He took out a Polaroid camera and a ballpoint pen, which he placed on the desktop. Then he stood up. 'For the passport photograph and to fill in the missing details. Miss Jarratt has been practising and can copy the handwriting precisely.'

'And then what happens to her?' Stark asked.

'She also has an open ticket. Two seats have been

provisionally booked on the three o'clock flight. I thought that travelling in the company of another would add to the deception. But if you prefer—'

'Send her up on your way out, Mr. Groves,' Stark interrupted. 'And keep on going.'

The Canadian went to the door. 'Until Toronto, then?'

'Maybe I'll see you,' Stark told him. 'If I do, I'll say thanks.'

'It is I who hope to be able to thank you, Mr. Stark.'

He went out, leaving the door open. He made no sound going down the stairs. There was a brief exchange of words in the passageway below, then the door opened and closed. Belinda came in through the doorway, swaying.

'We'll need to confirm the seats,' she said, coolly efficient.

'Do it.'

She used the telephone to call the Air Canada desk at Bromma Airport. She spoke in fluent Swedish to the linking operator, which explained how she had been able to hold down a cashier's job at the Ritz Hotel restaurant. When she broke the connection, she picked up the instant camera.

'Against the wall, I think?'

Stark shook his head and shrugged out of his jacket. 'Across the desk, darling.'

She was startled. 'What?'

'You. Across the desk. I used to have this fantasy about the dolly bird maths teacher at school. Naked skin against ink-stained wood.' He slid his tie out of the knot and started to unbutton his shirt. 'She was skinnier than you and didn't have a tan. But we never got much sun through the smog and high-rise flats in south London.'

Belinda swallowed hard. 'You mean you want me to . . .' She waved a hand over the desk. 'Here?'

'You tried the old-fashioned bedroom scene with a new twist, darling. But it didn't quite come off, did it?'

'But that was for a reason!' The big, dark brown eyes enlarged enormously as Stark removed his shirt and undervest in one movement. But when she saw his powerful chest with its matting of hair narrowing to a neat line running down his stomach, her tongue darted out to moisten her full lips.

'Now I've got a reason,' Stark muttered. He unzipped his fly, jerked down his trousers and underpants and straightened. He stood just on the fringe glow from the desk lamp. 'Like it to be hard on you.'

Belinda fastened her wide-eyed gaze on the point where his body hair thickened and spread. The image of her nakedness, vividly imprinted on his memory, aroused him to full readiness. 'Jesus Christ Almighty, this thing is getting wilder.' Watching Stark rather than what she was doing, she put the camera and papers on the swivel chair and the lamp on the floor. The area of the cone of light was further reduced and she stripped off her clothes in the semi-darkness even faster than she had done in Inga's bedroom. The sight of Stark's thrusting maleness and the act of undressing sparked her own arousal. Her nipples stood erect and her stomach moved in spasms as she stepped to the end of the desk. It was as if the foreplay with the Luger barrel was still reacting on her body, negating the need for further stimulation before the final penetration.

Because of her tallness there was no need to raise herself on to the desk. She simply rested her buttocks on the edge and lowered her back across the top. Her thighs parted in a wide vee and she held her arms high. Stark moved into the open tender trap of her legs and looked along the length of her body to her lust-heavy face. Her skin was sheened by the sweat of wanting again.

'Come on!' she urged hoarsely. 'The real thing must be better than the fantasy.'

He stepped up close to her, and thrust into her. Her warm, firm thighs encircled his back and tightened as she locked her feet. Then her hands found his neck and she pulled him down, his chest sinking on the soft twin cushions of her breasts with their hard centres. Her mouth crushed against his and then their lips parted. Her frantically working tongue sought to stretch into his throat as he clawed his fingers into her hair. His rigid maleness probed and retracted in the moist, sucking centre of her desire.

It was fast and it was frantic, her strong thighs crushing him ever-tighter until she tore her mouth away from his to moan the ecstacy of her orgasm. Stark was drained a moment later, shuddering into the liquid climax of an adolescent fantasy brought to reality. She allowed him to stand upright and pull out of her.

'Was it as good as you hoped it would be?' she asked breathlessly.

'Better,' he replied light-heartedly, with a matching grin. 'You smell good. The maths teacher always smelled of chalk dust.'

Belinda eased wearily up into a sitting position. She was not smiling. 'I'm glad you approve, Mr. Stark,' she said in her coldly efficient, secretary-to-employer tone. 'But I want you to know I'm not normally an easy lay. You had me because Mr. Groves asked me to co-operate with you.'

'Oh, hell!' Stark said with mock disappointment. 'And I thought it was because I had you over a barrel.'

CHAPTER THREE

BROMMA Airport is only about six kilometres west of Stockholm city centre and Stark planned to reach it just before check-in time to avoid a dangerously long wait in the departure lounge. Only a few minutes were used up by dressing in a dark blue worsted business suit and the trimmings from one of the suitcases. A few more in taking a Polaroid picture of himself and sticking it in the passport. He elected to call himself Frank Welles, after the maths teacher of his fantasy and a schoolfriend who had shared the same agony of the puberty period. Writing the name into the passport, on the airline ticket and across the traveller's cheques took only a matter of seconds.

Then they waited in idle silence in the semi-darkness of the spartanly-furnished office, Belinda in the chair and Stark squatting against a stained wall. When they did leave they made the trip in two unequal stages, both by taxi. The first cab from Karlavagen to the Central Station, where they had coffee before setting out on the second leg. The early-hour streets were for the most part deserted, the brilliant lighting seeming to expand their width, length and emptiness. Stark was as sure as he could be that they were not followed.

The airport complex buildings was the most crowded place they had been in since leaving the rented office. But it was the slackest period in the twenty-four hour cycle and Stark would have felt happier if there were ten times the number of transients to fill the light-dripping modernity of the departure lounge. He allowed a high-pressure porter to wheel the two suitcases from the taxi to the check-in counter. He followed the trolley, with a proprietorial hand cupped under Belinda's elbow. His eyes roved the bright surroundings with seeming nonchalance and he was disconcertingly aware of the smooth hang of his suit jacket. Both the Luger automatic and the S. & W. revolver were locked in the drawer of the rickety desk back in the office. Safe from discovery in anti-terrorist airport screenings – and of no use to Stark if he was spotted.

Belinda had some Swedish *Krone* and tipped the porter. Stark checked in the two suitcases with a comfortable five minutes to spare before the time limit expired.

'Hear that?' the girl asked as Stark turned her away from the scales set into the desk and steered her towards the entrance of the international section of the lounge.

The public address information system was broadcasting an announcement.

'Yeah, but I don't understand Swedish, remember?' he said.

The Swedish immigration officials looked at them and their passports with scant interest through weary eyes. The woman announcer translated the message into English:

'Air Canada regret to announce a delay in the departure of their flight AC-one-o-seven for Toronto via New York, scheduled to take off at three hundred hours. The delay is estimated at one-and-one-half hours.'

Check in time was an hour ahead of departure. The delay meant they had to spend at least two hours in the airport building before the first call to board.

'Maybe there's worse troubles at sea,' Stark said philosophically. 'Let's get some fags and booze. Act like ordinary passengers, darling.'

This section of the lounge was smaller. It held a proportionately smaller crowd of passengers, with hand baggage tagged for Alitalia, Transworld, British Airways and SAS flights as well as the Air Canada departure Stark and Belinda were to take. They visited the duty free shop, then bought some English-language newspapers and magazines from the newstand. Two uniformed policemen strolled in and out of the lounge from time to time, looking bored. Stark spotted four lone men he tagged as fake passengers. Like Belinda and himself they carried no hand baggage. He kept a surreptitious eye on them for thirty minutes before deciding they showed him no more interest than the other passengers. Probably security men on the prowl for potential hi-jackers. The company men put in an appearance after Stark and the girl had been seated on a padded bench in a corner for forty-five minutes.

Although she did not say anything, Stark guessed she had been infected by his coolly anxious caution. Like him, she merely went through the motions of reading the newspapers and scanning the picture magazines. But, while his attitude was one of relaxed watchfulness, she sat in rigid fear.

'Sorry you didn't go with the boss man?' he asked as he saw the four enforcers come through passport control and enter the international lounge.

'It's crazy,' she rasped. 'It was all like some sort of sad game before. Because Mr. Groves was so depressed and in desperate need of help, the danger didn't occur to me. Now the biggest risks are over. We're as safe as houses in here with all these people. Yet the way you're acting, like a gimlet-eyed G-man in one of those old movies, I'm so scared I'm almost wetting my pants. What the hell do plainclothes cops and company men look like? Maybe helping you look will keep my insides from spilling out.'

Stark grinned with his mouth. 'Coppers sometimes have big feet, but its not infallible. Mostly they have tired faces with wide-awake eyes. Some of them try to look tough and some of them are. None of them look like civil servants, which is what they are, basically. Think about them that way and they aren't so frightening. Company enforcers look like that four over there – don't stare at them, for Christ's sake!'

He leaned across in front of her to pick up the packet of cigarettes and box of matches from the table – and to block Belinda's expression of wide-eyed shock from the four men who were surveying the lounge.

'Them, I just smell,' Stark rasped.

He didn't, of course. It was the indefinable sixth sense that always warned him when a company enforcer was around:

strongly supported by the more concrete evidence of his eyes. Enforcers were literally the strength in the national arms of the multi-national company. The muscle, inevitably needing the guidance of somebody else's brain, which spearheaded the protection rackets, armed robberies, vice cover, murder and other unsubtle branches of crime which provided such a major source of income for the company. Another of their assignments was to stamp out the interference from trouble-makers both within and beyond the company. Thus had Stark been in close contact with the enforcers to a greater extent than any other company branch. And, because his survival depended upon it, he had quickly learned to detect when it was they, rather than he, who moved in for further contact.

Because it had begun in England,* he always thought of an enforcer, no matter of which nationality, as modelled on the British pattern. Tall and broadly built, but fast and smooth in movement. Hard faced with aggressive eyes. But, above all else, there was the incongruity of the man and his framework. Because of the basic requirements of his job, an enforcer never quite fitted comfortably into the shell of respectability which the company sought to maintain as a screen behind which to indulge its evil. Enforcers were thick-skulled roughnecks out-of-place under neat haircuts and inside expensive business suits.

'You mean they . . . actually are?' Belinda gasped, holding a copy of the *Illustrated London News* solidly in front of her face.

'It's six-to-four on,' Stark answered, lighting a cigarette with easy casualness. 'But I'm not going to get close enough for the clincher before I test out the bastards.'

She swallowed hard. 'The clincher?'

'The bulge, darling. Under the armpit, in the coat pocket, at the hip or in the small of the back. The gun bulge.'

He had not been aware of the Bromma security set up. The metal detection equipment was placed at the exit from

* See *The Revenger: Funeral Rites* (Sphere Books).

the lounge, through which passengers passed on their way to board the aircraft. He could have brought one or both the guns to the airport and ditched them here in the lounge when the Toronto flight was called.

'Sit tight, darling,' he muttered as he rose slowly to his feet, dismissing from his mind the regret over the missing guns. It was unimportant now. Just as it did not matter who had spotted him and given the word to company headquarters in Stockholm. The taxi driver, the porter, the check-in clerk, even one of the officials who had shown such cursory interest in their passports? Another passenger, a patrolling policeman or a security man? In addition to the full-time staff on its payroll, the company retained a network of casual informers. And with the bonus money – reward – put up by the international board for Stark's death or capture standing at a hundred thousand pounds sterling, countless pairs of eyes were peeled for him.

'What if they come for me?' Belinda rasped.

'Scream your head off, darling. Rape, or something. The company doesn't like trouble in public places.'

'Where are you going?' Her eyes told him that anywhere away from her was the wrong place.

'The room you're barred from,' he replied lightly, and headed for the door with the pictorial symbol for the men's lavatory. 'Get aboard as soon as they say the gate's open,' he called back to her.

With less time until departure he might have been prepared to sweat it out: sat and waited, challenging the enforcers to a public fraças. He doubted whether they were ready to break their own rule, even to take him out – company parlance for kill him. His assaults on them had already caused them to abandon the covering organisation of the multinational drilling and mining combine of Drake International, which had acted as a respectable front for every brand of criminal activity. But even so, they were not likely to toss aside everything that had made Drake work before Stark took a hand. The fact remained that large-scale organised crime integrated on a world-wide basis could not function in the face of intensive police scrutiny. And the police, while prepared to live with prostitution, narcotic pushing, protection, illegal gambling and fraud and corruption – which provided the largest percentage of company turnover – could do so only when official pressure was not brought to bear on them. Official heat was already on in Scandinavia, in the wake of the trail of carnage Stark left across Denmark and Sweden. So, as the company sought to pick up the pieces and get together a new front to replace Drake, they would be sure to operate more discreetly than ever to avoid attracting even greater attention.

But against this, Stark decided as he entered the wall-tiled, garishly lit lavatory, had to be set the top priority importance of taking him out. It was an operation that merited more than four enforcers. So, he had to believe that the quartet who had spotted him and were now moving towards the door he closed behind him, were just the first to arrive. Others would be speeding towards Bromma Airport, ready to invest in unwanted airline tickets to pass themselves into the international lounge. Maybe some fun-girls withdrawn temporarily from the vice circuit and even a few executives roused from their beds. Enough to swell the crowd of genuine passengers and provide a human screen behind which a quiet murder could be committed.

From experience, Stark knew that for him a crowded room could be as dangerous as an empty stretch of open countryside. In Cyprus there had been a café filled with people and noise, and then a deserted road in the Troodos Hills . . .*

In Stockholm there was a men's lavatory with somebody being sick in a cubicle, a lone user of one of the urinals and a bored looking attendant who had probably spent most of his sixty years overseeing other men's waste disposal problems. He just looked like somebody who should have been featured on the label of a disinfectant container.

* See *The Revenger: The Chinese Coffin* (Sphere Books).

The man at the urinal turned away, zipping up, and moved to a row of handbasins. The man in the cubicle made a lot of noise emptying his stomach. Taps sent a dual rush of water against porcelain. Stark strolled across the composition floor, then quickened his pace. The aged attendant sat on a cushion on a hard-seated stool at the open doorway of a small room. He looked up, pleased to be noticed, and said something in Swedish.

'English?' Stark asked, eyeing the room through the doorway. Shelves stacked with toilet rolls and paper towels. Buckets, brooms and mops in one corner. A bench supporting a jar of coffee, bottle of milk, packet of sugar, a mug, a kettle and a gas ring fed by a cylinder.

'A little. You wish for me to help you in some manner?'

Only the one door in the room. No way out of the lavatory except the one he had used to enter. The old man in the white coat began to rise from his stool.

'Yes,' Stark said. He gripped the scrawny upper arm of the attendant and backed him fast into the room. His free hand clamped over the slack mouth just before it could emit a cry of alarm. He backheeled the door closed after a glance over his shoulder showed the man at the washbasins dousing his face with water. The room had no windows. Just a fish-eye spy-hole in the door – to watch for toilet-roll stealers and graffiti poets? The air smelled strongly of disinfectant, a lot of the taint emanating from the old man's starched coat.

'Stay quiet and stay alive!' Stark rasped close to his prisoner's ear. Then he released him and swung around to put his eye to the spy-hole.

'You are Black September or something?' the old man asked tremulously.

'Maybe,' Stark told him.

The attendant began to whisper fast in his native tongue. The words had the tone of a prayer. It was a grotesque view through the fish-eye lens. A three hundred and sixty degree image of almost the entire lavatory – three walls, ceiling and floor; all in a curving perspective. The man at the washbasin and the four who moved in a tight-knit group through the door looked liked dwarfs imaged in a fairground's crazy mirror. All the enforcers had a hand tucked under a jacket lapel. Inside the cramped room, sounds from outside arrived muffled. A public address speaker in the lavatory issued an announcement. The name British Airways sounded clearly amid the string of Swedish words. Two of the enforcers strolled with forced nonchalance towards the urinals while the other pair explored the cubicles as if looking for ones which took their fancy.

When one of the doors opened and a wan-faced man looking shattered from his nausea staggered out, all four enforcers whirled towards him, hands diving deeper under their jacket. The announcement of the British Airways flight to Manchester being loaded for take-off began in an English translation. The man at the washbasin dried his face hurriedly on a roller towel and scuttled in the wake of the passenger who had been sick. The enforcers waited until the main door swung closed, then all concentrated their attention on the cubicles. It would take them only moments to check every one and find them empty.

Timing was essential to the success of Stark's plan. A lot of things could go wrong, but then that was invariably the case when the action was triggered by the enemy. The quartet of bulky, well-dressed men had half completed their cubicle search when Stark whirled from the spy-hole, pushed past the muttering old man and snatched up the gas cylinder. It could have been empty. But there could have been another way out of the lavatory in addition to the main door. Luck broke in all directions. Stark accepted the good and was always prepared to make fast alternative plans when fate turned sour on him. The outlet valve was partially opened and gas hissed angrily when he ripped the rubber pipe away from the ring inlet.

'Stay in here and say one for me,' he rasped at the old man as he lifted the cylinder. He checked the fish-eye lens.

The enforcers were overlapping along the uniform row of cubicle doors. Most of the time all he could see were their backs as they kicked open the doors, a hand always under the jacket. They were almost at the end, where they would turn and realise the attendant's room was the only hiding place left.

He leaned against the door, held the cylinder between his knees, turned the valve to release full pressure and struck a match. The gas smelled like rotten eggs. The hiss of its escape down the small bore pipe was loud and enraged for a brief moment. The roar of the flame was lower pitched, but angrier. It was bright blue and red, spurting at the nozzle, then flaring. Eighteen inches from start to finish.

Stark hefted the cylinder under his arm, swung the door wide and lunged outside. A whole 'plane-load of passengers breaking their necks for a pee might have been crowding into the lavatory. Or even one of the armed Swedish coppers. But the bad luck which had brought him into the trap, now smiled on Stark. There was just him and the four enforcers. They had completed their search and were glowering at each other as they turned away from the final empty cubicle. The distance to them from where Stark burst into sight was some twenty-five feet. The crash of the opening door, the roar of the gas flame and the beat of Stark's running feet snapped their eyes towards him.

The shock of seeing him and terror of the flame froze the enforcers for long enough to allow Stark to cover half the distance. Then three of them snatched their guns from the shoulder holsters. All Walther PPK automatics with the actions unset.

'Surrender, Stark!' the man who did not have a gun in his hand barked.

He was in charge. The other three were scared into fumbling as they worked shells into the breeches of the Walthers. Stark knew that they wouldn't give a shit for any no-shooting order when they felt the heat of the gas flame. He ran closer. The top man drew his gun. Another small automatic, but a Beretta ·38 for a change. Perhaps the other three saw the move and accepted it as a signal. More probably they acted in unified independence. They squeezed the triggers.

Stark dived forward out of the sprint. Bullets cracked over him and sprayed splinters from shattered wall tiles. The cylinder slipped from under his arm, clanged against the floor and tried to drag the rubber pipe out of his grip. He held on and jerked. Momentum slid him across the polished floor. The enforcers were still in a tight-packed, crooked line. Their guns swung down towards him. He directed the flaming pipe nozzle at their gun hands. One bullet snagged his jacket and another gouged into the floor. The other two men dropped their guns with agonised screams. Then the bright flame seared the hands of the next pair. A third Walther and the Beretta hit the floor. One man's coat sleeve was on fire. He flung himself into a cubicle and thrust his arm down the toilet bowl. The other three clutched at their burned hands with their good ones. Stark was still on the floor. Just before the men could break to scatter, he jerked at the cylinder again. Then pushed the slack pipe high and brandished it. Screams that had become moans exploded at shrill full-pitch again. Two of the men crumpled to their knees. Another staggered towards the washbasins. Blisters from the intense heat erupted immediately on their seared faces. Their hair and clothing were alight. They beat their arms and flailed their legs. They rolled and twitched.

Stark heard a roaring and a distant shouting as he sprang to his feet. As he tossed the cylinder with the still-flaring nozzle into the cubicle where an enforcer hung over the toilet bowl, he thought the sounds were inside his head. But then, as he raced towards the door, he realised it was a public address announcement against the background roar and whine of a jet-liner skimming into a landing over the roof of the airport building.

'Get a cup of coffee from the ladies, dad,' he called to the old man as he reached the door. Behind him, the enforcers were venting their agonies with moans again. He smoothed down his jacket where the dive had rumpled it, jerked open the door, stepped out and closed it quickly. Only Belinda Jarratt was looking towards him. No sound from inside the lavatory penetrated into the lounge. A lot of passengers sat and stared into space. Others read. Some dozed. A stream shuffled in an orderly line to pass in front of the metal detection equipment on their way to a boarding gate. The woman announcer aired her perfect English again, warning that this was the final call for passengers booked on the British Airways flight to Manchester.

Stark moved casually to join the line. Nobody was looking at boarding cards. Maybe they had a stewardess on the ramp to check them. He was being scanned by the electronics when the aged attendant ran from the men's lavatory, shrieking in high-pitched Swedish. With his watch removed, the equipment gave a negative result to Stark's examination. The two uniformed cops ran towards the lavatory door. The rubber-necks gathered around and the security men had to elbow their way through the crush. A stewardess gave Stark his watch and pointed absently in the direction of a group of straggling passengers headed for the boarding gate. She, the man operating the equipment and the passengers awaiting screening were all trying to see the cause of the excitement. Another stewardess, guarding the gate, was checking boarding passes.

An unmarked door opened easily when Stark turned the handle. It offered the only cover along the thirty feet of broad corridor between the first and second check-point. Stark groaned when he closed the door and switched on the lights. Then he grinned.

'When you gotta go, you gotta go, mate,' he told himself and went into a cubicle. It was one of only two and there was just a single washbasin. A lavatory for staff use, he guessed, from the absence of a sign on the door.

He locked the door, urinated in the bowl, then lowered the lid and sat down to wait. He smoked three cigarettes. Once the cubicle next door was used. The user, unaware he had not been alone, turned out the lights when he left. The darkness had the effect of dragging out the period of inactivity. It ended when he heard the second call for the Air Canada flight. Then it was just a matter of listening for the sound of many feet shuffling along the corridor outside, flushing the cistern and stepping out into the group of passengers. A few disinterested glances were cast at him. But it was the early hours of the morning, and the effect of the delay on pre-flight nerves wearied the travellers even more. Still keyed-up from his attack on the four enforcers, Stark was probably the freshest passenger to board the seven-o-seven.

Belinda was already in the window seat, her belt fastened and her eyes tightly closed, when Stark sat down next to her. He guessed she had been among the first to board. When she swung her head towards him and opened her eyes, they expressed shock rather than relief. A gasp escaped her lips.

'Jesus Christ Almighty, I thought you were gone for good,' she rasped in a harsh whisper as people nudged and shoved their way along the aisle searching out their seats.

'The original bad penny, darling,' he told her, grinning.

'There's got to be a stronger word than bad to apply to you!' she accused with soft vehemence. 'Those poor men!'

'It was them or me,' he replied, his tone still light and his mouth-line retaining its good humour. 'And I wouldn't be any use to the boss man bleeding to death back there.'

Some of the contempt for him drained out of her freckled face. 'All right,' she allowed, swinging her head to stare at the back of the seat ahead of her. 'But do you have to look as if you enjoyed it so much?'

'Why not?' Stark replied. 'It was quite a gas.'

CHAPTER FOUR

THEY didn't talk at all during the transatlantic flight. Belinda slept fitfully and Stark for a solid seven hours, she telling the stewardess not to disturb him for meals and light refreshments. Thus, the only new fact she discovered about him during the long, monotonous flight through the constant brightness of a static dawn was that, in repose, the set of his features suggested he might once have possessed a gentle side to his nature. But, the moment an abrupt drop into an airpocket woke him, every hint of what may have been was wiped away. He returned to instant awareness, his facial muscles working on the mask of hardness and his eyes raking the immediate surroundings to check all was well. The airliner regained its cruising height and the engine note resumed its regular beat of easy power. Belinda invited no conversation and Stark offered none. He went first to the washroom to freshen up, but had nothing to shave with. Then she moved down the 'plane and returned with fresh make-up on her face which did not conceal the worried look.

During the short New York stop-over they stayed aboard and she broke the long verbal silence, telling him of the rumours which had spread in the aftermath of the trouble at Bromma Airport. The consensus of uninformed opinion was that guerrillas were responsible. Only the nationalities and organisations of those involved were in doubt. A story not given much credence was that four armed men had attempted to rob the courier of an Amsterdam diamond merchant returning to Holland with an illicit consignment of gems purchased in Stockholm. Stark guessed that this was the account given by the quartet of enforcers. To have admitted they were gunning for John Stark would have dragged the company deeper into the mire of bad publicity: and put the four men beyond the pall of the expensive and extensive legal aid which would be theirs as long as they kept their mouths shut on the truth.

The stop-over at Kennedy Airport and then the flight north allowed full daylight to catch up with and overtake the Boeing. It was mid-afternoon when the airliner touched down to end its trip north-west of Toronto. Beyond the customs hall there was the usual crowd of expectant-faced people awaiting incoming passengers. Some of them, in chauffeur uniforms and in mufti, held signs to identify themselves to strangers they were to collect. Stark raked his eyes over all the faces: more than once. If the company was there waiting for him, it wouldn't be the first time he had escaped one country by the skin of his teeth, only to be met by more trouble in response to a coded cable or telephone message.

'There's Mr. Groves' man!' Belinda exclaimed, suddenly gleeful after the protracted period of taciturn ill-humour.

Stark put it down to the fact that she was back on home ground and had seen a familiar name. This name was neatly lettered in thick black strokes on a length of white laminate: GROVES INDUSTRIES CAR. It was held by meaty hands across the broad chest of a tall man with a dull-looking face beneath the shiny visor of his grey chauffeur's cap. His uniform was grey, too. With stay-bright buttons which, Stark noted, also carried the Groves Industries name when he got close enough to see.

'You're waiting for us,' Belinda told the man excitedly. 'Miss Jarratt and Mr. Welles?'

When the man smiled, he no longer looked dull. Instead, bright and intelligent.

'I surely am, Miss Jarratt,' he answered, tucking the board under one arm and touching his cap peak. 'I'll take those, Mr. Welles.'

He accepted the suitcases into his massive hands as if they were boxes of chocolates. He enjoyed getting them and they were no weight to carry.

'Just follow me. Car's right outside.'

He had an enforcer's build and in the chauffeur's uniform

there was no out-of-character framework by which to judge him. But, strolling alongside the girl in the wake of the big man, Stark grinned quietly at his own suspicion: while allowing that to stay alive he had to expect the worst at all times.

The car was a white Pontiac Executive station wagon, its cellulose and chromium trim glinting in the bright, warm sunlight. It had gold crests on the tailgate and front doors featuring a lot of detailed symbols above the Groves Industries name. The chauffeur had parked the car in a restricted zone immediately outside the exit doors of the arrivals building and a traffic cop was giving it the evil eye.

'Can we move fast, folks?' the chauffeur asked cheerfully, swinging open the nearside rear door. 'Some of these cops who get shoved out on the airport detail are so dumb they can't read.'

Belinda slid on to the plush seat, flashing a lot of tanned thigh, then Stark got in beside her. The chauffeur tossed the suitcases through the tailgate.

'Groves is a pretty important man around Toronto?' Stark asked.

The chauffeur got behind the wheel and gunned the car away from the kerb fast, flashing a triumphant glance at the rear-view mirror.

'And in Montreal, Winnipeg, Regina, Calgary, Vancouver and a lot of smaller cities you wouldn't have heard of,' Belinda replied with unconcealed pride. 'He's into plastics, fabrics, packaging materials and light engineering.'

'What are you into with him?'

'His confidential secretary.' She said it with a finality of tone which made it plain she was not prepared to elaborate.

The big car had tinted windows to keep out the sun's glare and air-conditioning to hold its heat and Toronto's pollution at bay.

'We're not going into the city?' the girl asked the chauffeur when she had got her bearing and realised they were heading north.

The metropolitan sprawl of Toronto was spread to the east and south along the shore of Lake Ontario. Most of the airport traffic had turned in that direction. The station wagon was barrelling along a stretch of four-lane dual-carriageway at the legal maximum. A directional sign proclaimed they were heading for Barrie, Lake Huron and Sudbury.

'No, Miss Jarratt. Mr. Groves said to take you and the gent up to a place south of Lake Nipissing.'

She looked puzzled for a few moments, then shrugged and relaxed back into the seat padding. 'You don't mind if I go to sleep, Mr. Welles. I didn't get much on the 'plane and it's more than a hundred and fifty miles to where we're going.'

'I'll wake you if anything exciting happens,' he promised wryly.

'With your brand of excitement I wouldn't know the difference,' Belinda told him sourly. 'It could be a bad dream.'

'Or a fantasy.'

In broad daylight, half a world away, the memory suffused her face with the bright red of harsh embarrassment. She bared her teeth in a silent snarl, then jerked her head around to curl up in the far corner of the wide seat. Stark met the knowing eyes of the chauffeur, imaged in the rear-view mirror, and gave him a grin. The man responded to the good humour. He didn't know the details but he could guess the general outline.

'Women!' Stark said.

Because a chauffeur was lower down the Groves Industries scale than the secretary to the boss, the man at the wheel confined his agreement to a silent wink. Stark looked out of the window at the southern triangle of the Province of Ontario wedged between the Great Lakes of Huron, Erie and its namesake. Clear of the Toronto environs the highway thrust and curved through a rich agricultural belt featured with immense wheat fields and rolling meadows on which herds of cattle grazed.

It was his first trip to North America, but Stark was blasé

about foreign travel. The roots of this attitude could be traced back to a period of his life before the company sank its claws into him – and he scratched back with far more ferocity. His love affair with high speed had led him into a job delivering expensive, custom-built cars all over Europe. He discovered then that one mountain, one lake, one strip of coast or one city centre was much like all the others. Only the language and the weather were different. But the novelty of punching a rich man's toy along a ribbon of road under all conditions had never worn off. Only the car and the road had mattered. Now, as the Revenger, only the means to kill and the victim were important. It was immaterial whether the environment was a back street in his native London on a wet winter night or the Côte d'Azur basking in summer sun.

The Pontiac made three stops. Twice to have its tank filled and once when Belinda woke up and said she needed the ladies' room. This last was at a roadside diner on the stretch of the Trans-Canada Highway between Orillia and Parry Sound. The chauffeur went into the diner for a Coke after asking Stark if he wanted one and getting a negative response. Belinda emerged first, looking out-of-place in her mini dress and high-heeled shoes against a background of open countryside.

'He's using the telcphone,' she said as she slid back into the car. All her old make-up had been wiped off and she had applied some fresh. The nap in the car had also helped her appearance. Stark had not realised how wan-faced and harrowed she had looked before.

The chauffeur came out of the diner whistling cheerfully. 'Mr. Groves ain't reached the lodge yet,' he said as he slid behind the wheel. 'Couldn't get any reply.' He started the motor and put the automatic shift into drive. 'Last leg of the long trip, folks.'

'I suppose he'll be using one of the company helicopters to get from Montreal?' Belinda suggested.

'I wouldn't know, Miss Jarratt. I just got the instructions

to meet you and the gent at Toronto and drive you up to the Nipissing Lodge. And to call when we were getting close.'

Stark eased his doubts about the chauffeur into high gear and tried to ignore the girl's use of the word *company*. It was natural for her to refer to Groves Industries thus. And maybe there was nothing odd about the telephone call.

The Pontiac continued to make good speed along the broad, main highway, the roadside signs always indicating that the next major city on their route was Sudbury. The vast area of water which was the Georgia Bay section of Lake Huron lay on their left. To the right the country was a pastoral mixture of farmland and forest. Then the chauffeur made a right turn on to a two-lane blacktop and the speed fell away as the road cut a tortuous route through heavily wooded country featured at irregular intervals with tiny communities clustered around sawmills. Afternoon faded into evening and Belinda asked for the air-conditioning to be turned off. She cracked open a window and gave a sensuous sigh as she breathed in the fresh scent of pine mixed with a pleasant aroma of new sawdust. The natural chill of the air had a healthier feel than the sterile stream which had been pumped into the car by the cooling unit.

'There it is folks,' the chauffeur announced in his usual bright and breezy tone.

The blacktop emerged from the timber at the crest of a hill. It was almost seven and the sun was still yellow, despite its nearness to the western horizon. It shimmered on the surface of the lake, visible in patches through fir trees perhaps five miles away. The lodge was much closer, no more than a mile distant. It remained in view as the Pontiac swooped down the hill, then cut off the blacktop on to a hard-packed dirt road that forked away to the right. There were two buildings, one large and one much smaller. Both were single-storey and constructed on the log cabin pattern. The faded lettering on a leaning sign at the start of the dirt road announced: *Lake Riding Lodge Only*.

The lodge was suffering from old age and lack of maintenance. The road approached it down a gentle slope which had been cleared of timber, probably to build it. The stumps of trees were covered by moss. Beyond the house and stable barn which faced each other across a rutted area tufted by clumps of weed, the timber grew thick and lush. A couple of windows in the house were smashed and cobwebs were meshed over the holes. The porch sagged and the door stood ajar. The barn leaned drunkenly to one side and its big door had fallen off the hinges and lay rotting on the ground.

It looked like the ideal place to hold a secret meeting. And it was good for a few other things, too. Stark didn't like it and sensed something was wrong. He knew he should be able to spot it, but it eluded him. He shot a sidelong glance at Belinda and saw she was eyeing the derelict buildings with distaste. The chauffeur drove the Pontiac into the yard midway between the house and the barn and eased it to a halt without locking the wheels. The dust kicked up by the big tyres settled as he slid out of the driver's seat.

'Ain't much, but I guess somebody called it home sometime,' he announced cheerfully as he sprang open the rear door on Belinda's side. He helped the girl out, then went to open the tailgate for the luggage.

'Aren't you supposed to wait?' the girl asked, eyeing the brooding silence of the house. Close up, the dereliction of the lodge had an eerie quality.

Stark was not concerned with imagination. He surveyed the house, the barn and the impenetrable curtain of trees with low-lidded eyes: tensely aware that he was open to attack from three sides with only the station wagon for cover. After the engine had been quiet for a few moments, the birds among the trees took up their interrupted evening chorus. The trilling innocence of the sound seemed to ease Belinda's doubts. The chauffeur's words continued the process.

'Surely am, Miss Jarratt. Mr. Groves said I was to wait with you if we got here first. Then I think I've got to drive you over to the Montreal apartment.' He put the suitcases down beside the car. 'Didn't say where Mr. Welles was to go from here. Guess someplace with Mr. Groves, uh?' He snapped a thumb and finger. 'Hell, almost forgot. Got a package for the gent in the glove compartment.'

Stark knew what was wrong. The realisation hit him just as the chauffeur leaned into the front of the car – there was no telephone line connected with the lodge. The overhead wire continued on along the blacktop with no spur down the dirt road. But he was ten feet away from the car, his back to it as he examined the house. He whirled, expecting to see the big man with the uniform snatching a gun from the Pontiac's glove compartment. Instead one of the meaty hands was turning the ignition key. The other was fisted around the automatic shift.

Belinda was staring at Stark, shocked by the brutal expression of anger which contorted his features. Then the roar of the big eight-cylinder engine exploded terror across her face. She spun around with a cry as Stark lunged forward. But the distance was too great. The chauffeur swung his legs into the car and stomped on the accelerator pedal. The parking brake had never been on. The rear wheels raced for traction, billowing dust, as the transmission was thrust into reverse. The pungent stench of exhaust fumes mixed with the taint of friction-burned rubber. Then the tyre tread found grip and the big station wagon plunged backwards out of the yard. The tailgate was still open, gaping like the jaws of some ravenous animal. The flapping rear door sent the two suitcases skittering. The chauffeur, craning to look over his shoulder, reached out to slam his door.

Stark pulled up sharply, cracking his eyes against the dust and choking on the million arid motes sucked into his throat.

'Jesus Christ Almighty, what's happening?' Belinda shrieked.

She stared after the wildly reversing car as it bounced and veered on the uneven track, tailgate and rear passenger door flapping. Stark's brain worked coolly. There was no danger from the retreating car or the direction in which it fled. The threat was in the barn, the house, the trees or all three.

He saw a spurt of dirt kicked up two feet to his left a moment before he heard the crack of the high velocity rifle. The direction of the disturbed dirt caused Stark to swing his gaze towards the trees. A muzzle flash and a puff of grey smoke splashed against the dark green of the foliage. High up among the branches. More dirt spurted, closer to him.

'Move it!' he yelled to the girl, and whirled to lunge at the house. It was closer than the barn.

Belinda screamed as the crack of the second shot sounded above Stark's command. Then she sprinted after him, pausing only to kick off her shoes. One of them hit the ground under Stark's running feet. His sole slid off the long heel and into a rut. He pitched forward with a curse and smacked into the ground with a grunt. A jarring pain exploded in his elbow and travelled the length of his arm in both directions. Bullets whined over his sprawled form. Belinda raced past him, trailing a wail of terror. Stark went up on to all fours and a bullet smacked into the ground between his splayed hands. He couldn't hear the throb of the Pontiac's engine anymore. The sound of his breathing was loud in his ears. His injured elbow gave way and he rolled to the side. The sniper had a fast-action rifle. And it had a multi-round magazine. Bullets whined around him. Always close, but never close enough. The idea hit Stark that the rifleman was not aiming to kill him: not with a rifle anyway. As he forced himself up on to his hands and the balls of his feet again, he caught a glimpse of the Pontiac. It was no longer racing away in high-speed reverse. Instead it was parked, bodytrim gleaming in the fading light of the dying sun, halfway up the slope. The chauffeur was out of the car, leaning on the door, looking down on the scene. Like an idly interested spectator at a clay-pigeon shoot.

Belinda's bare feet drummed on the wooden porch of the house. A shot followed her gasp of relief as her shoulder thudded into the partially open door. Then Stark knew why the sniper was firing so many shots without hitting anything but dirt. The door plunged open and triggered a detonator. An ancient rainwater barrel was standing three feet back from the threshold. In one horrendous instant it released the full power of its tightly-packed contents of plastic explosive and sawn up pieces of an old car bodyshell.

Stark was leaning forward in a crouch when the explosion boomed. It took the smallest part of a second for the thrust and heat of the blast to reach him. In that tiny fragment of time, he saw Belinda Jarratt transformed from a vital human being into a charred piece of debris. Then, as the force of the blast lifted him off his feet and hurled him backwards, the seared remains of the girl disintegrated. He didn't see this. His eyes were tight closed against the heat and he curled his body into a ball, tucking his head hard to his chest in readiness for the inevitable impact. He probably lost consciousness for a short span of time. It took no longer for the actual explosion to expend itself. Searing blast and hurtling chunks of metal flattened the house. Belinda's dead, naked body with hair flaming and pieces of frazzled flesh dropping from it, was blown and ripped apart by the same destructive forces.

Stark's flying body held a low trajectory, smacked against the ground and bounced into the open doorway of the barn. The viciously scything, white hot shards of metal and the hail of blazing timber wrenched from the house flew upwards in higher arcs. Stark plunged deep into the life-saving cushion of a massive heap of rotten straw. The enormous thump of the explosion was still like a physical barrier around his aching head, blotting out the sounds of roaring flames and raining debris. And the ache seemed also to be something tangible, threatening to explode its way out of his skull. Intense enough to negate every other pain in his body. The heat of a thousand broiling days was trapped inside the pile of straw. Stark was illogically afraid he was going to drown in his own sweat. He didn't know where he was or what had happened. It seemed to take hours for a single vivid memory to trigger total recall. The rather pleasant contrast of puffs of grey smoke and flashes of orange against a dark green background.

'Move yourself, you lazy bastard!' he muttered. 'You've got company.'

CHAPTER FIVE

THE sniper dropped down from the branches of the pine tree, on to the roof of a pick-up truck, thence via the flatbed rear to the ground. He carried a German-made Kar 7·92mm rifle with a 22-inch barrel, fitted with a 4X telescope.

'Didn't I say I'd rig the best damn booby trap you ever saw in your damn life?'

The sniper was a stockily built man in his early twenties dressed in blue jeans and a check shirt. He had the kind of embittered face upon which a smile would look incongruous. The man who spoke so excitedly and rubbed his hands together in glee was at least double the sniper's age. He was dressed in much the same way, with the addition of a straw hat loaded with dry flies around the brim.

'Another magazine,' the sniper demanded clicking out the old one.

The happy man leaned inside the open passenger door of the battered Chevrolet pick-up and jerked out a rucksack. He got a fresh magazine from under the flap and watched eagerly as it was snapped into place.

'Won't be nothin' but pieces of torn up house to shoot at after my damn bomb went off!'

'Button it, George!' the sniper snarled. 'Cat's got nine lives. This cat's got more than that, the number of times guys have tried to take him out.'

'Aw, you're nothin' but a damn pessimist,' George groaned, trailing the sniper through the trees.

They emerged from the timber just as the Pontiac rolled to a halt on the far side of the yard. The chauffeur couldn't bring it any closer because of the scattering of charred debris which had been spewed by the explosion. If there was any part of Belinda Jarratt's disintegrated body in sight it was unrecognisible from the shattered chunks of house timber. Any blood she had spilled had been evaporated by the intense heat. Flames continued to flicker among the foundations of the house, supplementing the fading light of the sun penetrating the dispersing pall of black smoke.

'Some bomb, uh?' George yelled across the yard.

'Couldn't you have saved just a little of the stuff?' the chauffeur answered wryly. 'Mr. Essex might want you to blow a hole in Niagara Falls next week.'

George giggled with near hysterical pleasure.

'You see what happened?' the sniper wanted to know sourly as he picked his way delicately through the debris, as if afraid to get his heavy work boots dirty.

The chauffeur moved forward for a meeting at the centre of the yard. 'The broad got it full frontal. Torn to pieces, I figure. Too much smoke and flame to see what happened to Stark.'

The sniper spat. 'The frigging mad bomber got too enthusiastic.'

'Jealous is all!' George said happily, raking his tiny eyes proudly over the ghastly results of his explosive device.

'Mr. Essex is going to want more than just our word Stark is spread over the country in a hundred different directions.' He pivoted into a complete slow turn, the barrel of the German rifle covering the same ground as his eyes. He halted the movement, stiffened, and stared. The smile on his face showed as a sneer. 'Hey, there he is.'

He thrust the rifle forward, towards the entrance of the stable barn. The familiar grey of Stark's suit showed against the yellow of the straw in the half light beyond the wide doorway. Just the back of the jacket and the tops of the legs were visible. Stark's head and shoulders and his legs up to the knees appeared to be sunk into the straw.

'Hold it!' the sniper snapped as George made to run towards the barn.

He jerked the rifle to his shoulder, sighting along the side of the telescope rather than through it. George recalled what his partner had said about Stark having more lives than a cat and he held back cautiously: did not start to advance until the sniper was in front of him and the chauffeur beside him.

'Wouldn't it be just terrific if he's still alive?' he said in a whisper. 'I reckon the board will give us more than the quarter of a million bucks if we bring him in still breathing.'

'Button it!' the sniper rasped, sweating with the tension of having Stark at the wrong end of a gun; and the excitement of picking up his share of the bonus money. George could just be right about the international board of company executives upping the ante for a live prisoner.

He wanted silence so that, as he entered the barn, he could hear if Stark was still drawing air into active lungs.

Stark was, but he was doing it silently. It wasn't easy, because his lungs seemed to be crushed by caved-in ribs and on fire from the red hot blast he had sucked into them. Every other organ, bone, tissue and nerve ending in his body gouged at him to give vocal outlet to its agony. Instead, he squatted in utter silence on a narrow beam that ran along inside the front wall of the barn, immediately above the entrance. On either side of him other beams ran in the opposite direction beneath the angle of the roof. At the rear, above the stable stalls, they were boarded to form a hayloft. But at the front the beams were just the skeleton of a ceiling. Stark was dressed in shoes, socks, underpants, shirt and tie. His suit was below, hurriedly stuffed with some of the straw from the heap on which it rested. In broad daylight, the dummy human form would not have fooled anybody. But in the semi-dark interior of the barn with the outside light fading fast, it drew the three company men into the barn.

The sniper came first, his rifle probing out in front of him. Stark held his breath then, and poised himself. He waited just long enough to see that George and the chauffeur were not holding guns. Then he powered down from the beam. In both hands he held the long wooden handle of a pitchfork. One rusty tine had been broken off long ago. But the other was still in place, curving down to a blunted point. The weight of Stark's falling bulk and the force with which he drove the pitchfork ahead of him compensated for the bluntness of the tine. The rusted length of metal burst through the hirsute flesh at the nape of the sniper's neck. It continued to probe downwards, grating along the vertebrae of the man's spine as it ripped through the spongy tissue.

The man screamed like a pole-axed animal and pitched forward. He had fully nine inches of metal buried in him and his nervous system could not stand the shock. It seized up and the sniper was dead before he banged his face against the ground. The rifle was under him and Stark ignored it. He already had a weapon in his hands and he wrenched it clear. A single short, deluge of blood spouted from the wound. The tine of the pitchfork had been bent into almost a right angle by the weight of the falling body. The blood was redder than the rust, and spots of it flicked through the air as Stark whirled.

If both George and the chauffeur had been armed, Stark would certainly have died. Had one of them been able to pull a gun, it was likely the Revenger's fate would have been sealed. For, although the company men were rooted to the spot for stretched seconds, unable to do more than stare at the half-dressed apparition with the blood-dripping weapon, Stark did not have the strength to continue the attack. He swayed and the pitchfork sank into a decaying arc, swinging towards the men with its own momentum. But the mere sight of the red-run prong heading for them snapped George and the chauffeur out of their state of shock. And, with no guns, they could only whirl and race across the debris-scattered yard.

Stark allowed the pitchfork to hit the ground, and leaned against it. Something was wrong with his eyes. It was as if pain had become a physical force once more. His mouth refused to open in a scream, so it flooded into his eyes in search of escape. They blurred and it seemed as if the fleeing men were swimming through misty water towards the parked Pontiac. Stark blinked, then groaned. His vision cleared and he saw the men getting into the car. His pain-wracked mind became convinced there was an arsenal of weapons in the station wagon. The men were going to get them and blast him into eternity. Like they blasted Belinda Jarratt.

'You got paid out for all that blaspheming you did, darling,' he said, his voice helping to keep him conscious. When he hurled aside the pitchfork, his support was gone. He fell hard on to his bare knees. 'You got a bigger bang out of the explosion than from the Luger!' He giggled uncontrollably as the car doors slammed. 'Your fault. I warned you anyone gets close to me they're liable to end up dead before their time.' He yanked at the barrel of the Kar rifle. The telescopic sight snagged on the sniper's shirt. 'Or did I say that to Inga?' He used a foot to roll the dead man off the gun. The Pontiac's engine came to life with a powerful roar.

He didn't need to talk to himself anymore. They were company men out there and they were getting away. He couldn't let that happen. They had tried to kill him, but that was all right. They had killed Belinda. And another girl in Denmark . . . what was her name? A woman in a Bierut hotel. Amanda. And Carol! Most of all Carol. The start of it all. With different men doing the killing. But the same breed. A breed that threatened to over-run the whole world. Unless it was stamped out. And there was only him, John Stark, to do the stamping.

He was on his feet and staggering into the gaping doorway. Looking ridiculous, he thought, with the lengths of his legs showing bare between the flapping shirt tails and the socks at his ankles. He worked the Kar's action. It came easily to him. Since setting out on his mission of revenge he had come to have the same instinctive feel for guns as for cars. And he was as expert at handling them.

The Pontiac was barrelling up the slope, spewing dust from the spinning rear tyres. He leaned against the door frame, nestling the stock of the rifle against his shoulder. The bumping station wagon was out of focus through the telescope lenses. He waited for it to reach the top of the slope, when it became clearly defined. He aimed for the front offside tyre. In close up he saw the rent appear in the wide side wall. Saw the dust spurt under the escape of air. Saw the wheel turn as the rubber shreaded.

Then he looked with the naked eye. The car had stopped, canting to one side and forward. The doors folded open and the two men half fell out and powered into a run. They headed out in opposite directions, but both seeking to attain the crest of the hill. Stark rested his left eye against the telescope again and zeroed in on the chauffeur first. He was the faster man and leapt into close-up through the scope lenses. His fast movement and Stark's unsteadiness, made more apparent by the high-powered optics, hampered the shot. Stark hadn't noticed it when he aimed at the spinning tyre. The thought crossed his mind that he was not entirely the machine in human form he considered himself. Perhaps there was some glimmer of compassion deep inside him that altered his attitude when he was aiming at a man instead of an inanimate object.

Or perhaps it was a complete reversal of this theory. To kill was the name of the game he played and the depth of his desire to blast the life out of the running man was what made him a more difficult target than the tyre.

The hairline sights of the scope marked a cross in the centre of the chauffeur's back and Stark squeezed the trigger. He saw in vivid detail the effects caused by penetration of the 7·92 mm bullet. The hole through the smoothness of the uniform jacket, neat for an instant. Then, as the man pitched to the ground out of the lumbering run, an uneven patch of crimson blossomed around the hole. He smashed hard into the low brush among the moss-covered tree stumps and the impact spurted a gout of blood from the wound.

The shot at George had to be a fast one. The bomb expert who loved his work so much had reached the top of the hill and was going out of sight on the other side. The only vital target visible to Stark was the man's head and the trigger was squeezed as the hairline sights swept over the straw hat. The hat with its colourful decorations of dry flies spun off the head, but it was not all George lost. Because of the upward trajectory of the bullet, it slanted in through the back of his head and exited through the top of the skull. There was some less vividly coloured matter speckling the blood that gouted from the exit wound. George collapsed out of sight with his brains spattering the ground ahead of him.

Stark sagged against the doorpost and slid to the ground. The rifle slid from his hands. He was certain it had killed him as effectively as the two company men staining the hillside with their blood. The effort of holding and aiming it had drained his last reserve of strength and the thuds of its recoil against his shoulder had stomped the life from the final group of nerve-endings which had not been obliterated by the explosion.

But, although he felt oddly detached from himself, he did not lose consciousness. For a long time there was no pain. Just a complete numbness that would not allow him to move. All he could do was stay huddled at the foot of the doorpost, staring directly ahead at one particular spot amid the debris-strewn yard. His senses of sight, smell and hearing operated perfectly and he had the feeling that his brain was working smoothly enough to solve all the world's problems. But he couldn't be bothered with them. It was better, as the last of the fires burned out and the moon rose, to just sit and look at the displaced eye of Belinda Jarratt. And to wonder whether it was the left or the right one. The eye, glinting in the moonlight against the matt black of a sooted piece of metal, stared back at him in mute accusation.

'Don't blame me, darling,' he said, his voice a croak. 'It was Groves who invited you to this party. Still. I don't suppose even he knew it was going to be such a blast.'

CHAPTER SIX

RICHARD Corwin Essex felt reasonably confident as he shot a lonely game of billiards in the rumpus room of the duplex apartment on King Street East in downtown Toronto. The noise of the city, as the business day drew to a close and the night spots opened up, was just a hum within the apartment, which was more than a hundred and fifty feet above street level and protected by insulated walls and double-glazed windows. The Glenn Miller band oozed gentle swing in low volume from the hi-fi and the click of billiard balls colliding was as relaxing to the ears of Rick Essex as the music.

He was not an impressive figure as he moved around the full-size table in the spacious room, choosing his shots with care and leaning over the cue to hit them with easy skill. At fifty-two, he had all the signs of middle-age which had been allowed to encroach with no opposition. His stature was small – he stood five feet six inches tall and had narrow shoulders and a torso that had been wiry in younger years. But now his girth was disproportionately large so that the line of his bulging belly seemed to start at the neck and fall in a great, sagging curve to finish hanging over his belt. His once sandy hair was now predominantly grey and was thinning fast. The one consoling factor about the aging process, whenever he stopped to consider the effect of the passing years upon his appearance, was in respect of his face. It had never been either handsome or ugly: rather, an insignificant balance between the two extremes which defied any description apart from nondescript. But the deep lines scored into his flesh by time had added character to the features. Thus, the ordinary grey eyes, the well-chiselled nose and the soft-looking mouth set into his roundish head were given subtle interest by the network of tiny cracks which deepened, lengthened or changed direction according to the emotion he was expressing.

Mostly, as he knocked the two white and one red ball around the green baize, he showed intense concentration. And it was an expression he wore most of the time, for Rick Essex strove to achieve the optimum in everything he did – whether by way of relaxation or work. For the former, he engaged in games of skill and took handsome young men to bed. Such pursuits, he had discovered, provided the ideal means to unwind from his exacting work as top executive of the Canadian arm of the company.

His confidence as he shot the one-sided game of billiards was two-fold. First, he felt sure Danny Walker and the other two enforcers would successfully take out John Stark. And, secondly, he was certain he was going to beat his former highest break.

Rick Essex's confidence proved to be half well-founded. He reached a hundred and ninety and a few moments later purposely miscued to let the break stand at two hundred and four. By that time Danny Walker was dead – he was the sniper at Lake Riding Lodge.

Essex switched off the bright table lamps, killed the Miller cassette and went downstairs to the luxuriously furnished living room of the duplex. He didn't notice the time until after he had poured and drunk a stiff shot of Haig Pinch. Then he slid on his gold wrist watch and saw it was almost eight o'clock. Two hours since Walker had telephoned to say the hi-jacked Groves Industries car was within striking distance of the derelict lodge. Plenty of time for Stark and the girl to have been taken out and for all three enforcers to reach a telephone and report they had earned the bonus money. Essex poured another Scotch and shuddered when the liquor hit the spot.

Then he went to sit in the deep armchair beside the telephone table and began to chew on his nails. He waited and chewed for fifteen minutes, willing the instrument to bleep. It remained sullenly silent and he finally acknowledged he had been wrong to listen to Danny Walker. The boy wasn't going to place the call, so there could be no excuse about tying up the 'phone. He got up, went to the rough stone fake fireplace and pressed a phoney knot in the distressed timber beam which formed the mantelshelf. A section of the stone swung open and he squatted to spin the combination lock in the circular door of the safe. From the safe he took a black notebook and memorised a Sudbury telephone number. He resecured the safe, clicked the secret panel back into place and returned to the armchair. He dialled the number.

'Trans-Canadian Escort Service, good evening.' The man had a silkily smooth voice.

'Essex.'

'Yes, sir?' Curt, efficient and a little afraid now.

'We may have a problem in your area, Vic,' the man with the sagging belly said solemnly. 'The number one international problem.'

'You mean—' Very scared now.

'You know what I mean!' Essex snapped, cutting in before the man in Sudbury could name Stark over a public telephone link.

'He's in Canada?'

'Will you just listen?' Essex's irritation was mounting. 'A place called Lake Riding Lodge a couple of miles south of Nipissing. I don't know the local geography.'

'I'll find it, Mr. Essex.'

'Make sure you do – and fast. And alert the undertakers. Call me back at the Toronto duplex as soon as you've made a survey.'

He broke the connection without waiting for an acknowledgement. The lines cut into his round face deepened and lengthened to show anger mixed with resignation to defeat. For he was certain the undertakers would be needed: and to call up their services was to admit failure. The undertakers formed a specialist branch of the company: men – hardly ever women – whose job it was to clear up the mess left when an operation went wrong. And to do it fast before the public or police reached the scene and spotted signs implicating the company. Internationally they had become overloaded with work since John Stark had declared war on the company. Sometimes abiding by the literal meaning of their appellation by collecting and disposing of dead bodies. At other times removing evidence of destruction. Often it was a combination of the two.

It would take time for Vic Ainsworth in Sudbury to check out what had gone wrong and call back. Essex chewed his nails some more and contemplated issuing an Ontario alert for Stark – or even a coast-to-coast one. But he decided to hold off until he had eye-witness verification that such steps were necessary. After all, even if Stark had taken out the three enforcers, there was a possibility he had also bought it in whatever action happened up at the lodge. He moved away from the silent telephone, heading for the open drinks cabinet. Then he shook his head, chiding himself, and veered towards the stairway. He went up to the rumpus room and began throwing darts at the board, speaking aloud the numbered segments and hitting the chosen target each time. It helped to keep his mind off the gruesome image of Danny Walker's beautifully hard body growing harder as *rigor mortis* set in.

Stark drove the Chevrolet pick-up towards Toronto, back-tracking on the route taken by the Pontiac. Once on the main highway he was able to maintain a constant speed and the only movements he had to make entailed a gentle swing of the steering wheel one way or the other to negotiate bends in the road. Thus, able to sit more or less immobile in the comfortable cab of the speeding vehicle, he could rest his battered body. His mind, long immune to shock, was unaffected by the traumatic experiences at the lodge. It worked smoothly and to a large part automatically, assimilating road conditions and the signs which glowed with reflective paint in the wedge of yellow sprayed out by the truck's head-lights.

It had taken him thirty minutes to recover sufficiently to begin his preparations for leaving the scene of carnage at the lodge. Initially, any movement erupted white hot pain in every part of his body and he had to will himself to do what was necessary. But then the exercise isolated the main seats of agony to his right knee, both his shoulders and his left wrist. He thought he probably had bruising in many other areas but it was these joints which erupted groans from his lips whenever he asked too much of them. And too much was hardly anything at all. But at least he had no broken bones.

The will to fight the pain came from the knowledge that such a well-planned operation as the ambush and booby trap was not one which would have been taken in isolation by the three company men. Others would know of it and when a report was not received, a check would be run. So Stark worked as fast as he was able to get clear of the area.

First he located both the suitcases, which had been hurled twenty yards by the blast. They were battered, but had not burst open. He dressed in a clean shirt and a dark blue suit. A battery shaver took off most of his stubble. The Kar rifle was too complex to break down, but he found a ·38 Chief Special with a two-inch barrel in the sniper's pocket. He transferred it to his own. Then he got the passport and traveller's cheques from his old suit and went in search of the vehicle by which the sniper and George had reached the remote lodge. It didn't take long to locate the pick-up parked on a track running through the timber. In looking for the gun, he had already checked the sniper's pockets and found identification showing his name was Daniel Walker and he lived on Charles Street in Toronto. He had left that, but taken the billfold containing thirty-five dollars and a handful of loose change from his trouser pocket. The track out of the trees emerged on to the blacktop a mile east of the lodge, but Stark detoured back to where the bodies of George and the chauffeur were sprawled. He collected a further seventy-eight dollars and a little more loose change. The ready cash would be useful but was not the main purpose of his search through the dead men's pockets. He was looking for any pointers to company operations and personnel. All he got were two addresses, one in Toronto and the other in Sudbury.

He started the long drive back to the city, conscious that although the pick-up was painted a drab grey and carried no markings, it could well be on the stolen vehicles list. Or, alternatively, be a company-owned vehicle and recognisable as such. He stopped twice at service stations, but didn't leave the wheel. Neither of the pump attendants gave him a second glance. They filled up the tank, accepted payment plus tip and wished him a safe trip. And he had one.

He drove into Toronto on Bloor Street at ten to eleven by the dashboard clock and knew it was a dangerous time. The company must now be aware of what had happened at Lake Riding Lodge and the word would be out on him and the Chevrolet. And in such a criminally rich pickings city as Toronto the company would be strongly represented. Countless pairs of eager eyes would be looking for him and the Chevrolet. So he shortened the odds on discovery by ditching the pick-up. But not until he had turned left on to Yonge Street and driven closer to the crowded heart of the city. He left the vehicle, with the keys still in the ignition, on the Gerrard Street side of St. James Square and began to hoof it, carrying a suitcase in each hand. He immediately felt more secure for, unless there had been additional cover at the airport, every Canadian company man who had seen him was now dead.

Back on Yonge, walking south-east, he saw a billboard advertising the Windsor Manor Hotel which appeared to present a plush image. He would have preferred a more downmarket place, but his expensive luggage and high-price clothes would have made him conspicuous. The billboard said the Windsor Manor was on Front Street. The female part of a middle-aged couple emerging from the Downtown Theater told him Front Street was a cab ride away. An untalkative taxi driver took him there, moving through streets by turn well lighted and crowded and deserted and shadowed. The hotel was a new one, a white stone and polished glass multi-storey building between a business section and a bar and restaurant area. It catered for the tourist trade and out-of-town businessmen. Both groups of guests had to be rich. Stark had the appearance to make him acceptable at the desk and he chose a second floor single room with bath at the rear of the hotel from the selection of accommodation offered him. A bright-eyed bellboy showed him to the room, which was impersonally luxurious. His aching shoulders were relieved to be free of the suitcases as he followed the youngster.

As soon as he was alone, he checked the free opening of the window which overlooked the roof of a single-storey projection at the rear of the hotel. Probably the kitchen, or perhaps the staff quarters. The roof was flat and extended to the side street which ran parellel with Front. In offering him an easy way out of the room if he had to leave surreptitiously, it also extended an invitation to simple entry – apart from the fact that the window could be opened only from the inside.

The room had no television, but there was a radio built into the headboard of the bed. A programme guide on the writing bureau told him which station broadcast the most frequent news bulletins and he tuned in to this wavelength. It was oozing out canned, late-night music. Stark thought the undertakers would take care of the carnage at the lodge but there was always the chance that some innocent passer-by might have got there first. And called the police.

The music was interrupted at eleven-thirty as Stark lay on the bed, luxuriating in the softness of the mattress and the ease which inaction brought to his punished body. A monotoned newscaster read snappy reports of street accidents, a big factory fire on the lakefront, Middle East political moves and the latest on student unrest at the university. When the over-sweet music restarted, Stark turned off the radio and consulted the Toronto City telephone directory. There was no private listing for Groves, but four in the name of Groves Industries Incorporated. One address was the Groves Building on Adelaide Street West. The others were for plants spread over the north side of the city. He tried one of the factory numbers first, and got through to a man who sounded irritable and not too intelligent.

'Yeah, what do you want?'

'Like to know how I can get in touch with Mr. Groves,' Stark told him.

'Groves? Jesus. Against company policy to reveal employee's home addresses and telephone numbers. And Mr. Groves ain't just another employee, right?'

'It's important.'

'To you, mister. My job's important to me. Call the Groves Building on Adelaide in the morning.'

The connection was broken and the dialling tone burred. It had been a long shot and calling the Groves Building number was another one. He expected to hear the unanswered signal, or at best, the mechanical sound of a recorded announcement.

'Hello?' A man's voice, frightened and recognisable.

'Don't talk,' Stark said quickly, his estimation of the Canadian businessman going up a notch or two. At least Groves hadn't crawled into a hole somewhere to sweat it out. He had taken a positive step. 'You must know this is Belinda's travelling companion. We got mixed up with some bad company. I'm—'

'Belinda?' He spoke the name as though he considered it the most beautiful word in the English language.

'She got taken out.' There was no way to soften the blow, and he hurried on, anxious to say what he had to before the shock hit Groves and perhaps blotted out his mind to all else. 'I'm a bit under the weather. Be at that number at seven o'clock tomorrow morning. And have a place for a nice quiet meeting in mind.'

'But I—'

Stark rattled the receiver back on to its cradle, then dialled

O to get the desk. He asked for a seven-thirty call. Then he stripped, put the revolver under his pillow and got beneath the sheets. The pains took a few minutes to calm after the activity but once they had subsided to a bearable level, sleep came easily.

Rick Essex did not sleep. He was wide awake and concentrating hard. Not playing games now, but working. For the call had come in from Vic Ainsworth. Stark had struck his first blow against the Canadian arm of the company. Three enforcers dead, including Danny Walker, Essex's favourite lay in Toronto. Belinda Jarratt had also been killed but that was no compensation at all. The only good news Ainsworth had been able to report was that the undertakers had the situation under control: all signs of fatalities would be removed, the crippled car would be taken away and broken down into scrap and the lodge would have every appearance of being razed by a mystery fire.

All that was water under the bridge – as was the mistake Essex had made in not hedging his bet for taking out Stark.

'You were a goddamn fool, Rick!' Harry Gorman snarled. 'Letting that cocksucking punk tell you how to run this operation.'

Essex had been pacing the deep-pile carpet which spread wall-to-wall over the living room floor. He always found problems easier to solve when he was on the move. But now he halted and whirled to glare at the hawkish face of the man in charge of the day-to-day running of company affairs in the province of Ontario. Gorman was a tall, powerfully built man of forty-two with a beak-like nose, sharp eyes and an aggressively set jaw. It was common knowledge in the top echelons of the company that he was next in line to replace Essex whenever it proved necessary. And ever since he had achieved this distinction Gorman had ceased to conceal his low regard for the top man.

'It was my decision and mine alone!' Essex rasped angrily.

'It goddamn well shouldn't have been!' Gorman shot back.

'Stark lit down on my piece of territory. You ought to have consulted me before going off half-cocked.'

It was true. Essex had himself organised the Canadian arm's set up whereby each major province was under the control of individual executives subordinate only to him, with Nova Scotia, New Brunswick and Prince Edward Island grouped together as a single unit. It worked well and had the pleasing side effect of freeing Essex from much arduous paperwork. He could move about at will between the more than a dozen homes he maintained across the country. And the only distasteful chore he had to undertake in normal circumstances was assimilating the monthly reports filed by the top man in each province, which he then submitted to the international board's offices in Rome. Otherwise, it was only when infrequent trouble occurred that he involved himself in local matters.

'I had to move fast!' he rasped.

'You moved fast to try to make me look bad and grab all the goddamn glory for yourself!' Gorman retorted. 'And I'm goddamn glad it blew up in your fag's face!'

Gorman was sprawled in Essex's favourite armchair beside the telephone table. His shirt was crumpled and his necktie was askew. He was unshaven and his brown hair was uncombed. Although his eyes were bright, it was obvious he had been roused from bed and dressed hurriedly to come to the duplex.

'Stop griping and try to figure if there are any angles we haven't covered!' Essex told him, and started to pace again.

Arguments between the two men were pointless. Each knew the other hated his guts and there was nothing to be gained from labouring this point.

'I got good reason to gripe!' Gorman snarled. 'You let Stark stir the shit in my territory and that ain't gonna look good to the big boys.'

'I'll cover you, for Christ sake!' Essex answered, trying to moderate his tone, but striking the wrong note. It came out shrill – shrewish. Outside of the bedroom with a suitable partner, Essex only ever revealed overt signs of his homosexuality when he was needled into a temper.

'I'll goddamn make sure you goddamn do!' Gorman told him.

Essex allowed time to pass as he continued to pace, stressing his intention to ignore the implied threat. Then: 'You're sure we've got every available man on to this?'

Gorman sighed. 'And woman. In Toronto, Ottawa, Hamilton, London, Sudbury, Sault Ste. Marie and Oshawa.'

There was a Groves Industries plant in every one of these towns.

'And the word's out to every tip-off man. If Groves shows himself any place in southern Ontario, we'll know thirty seconds after the spotter reaches a 'phone.'

'I still say we should let Montreal know and put out an alert on Stark himself,' Essex argued.

'So let Montreal know,' Gorman allowed with a shrug. 'Let the whole goddamn country know and watch operations go into low gear while everyone turns over rocks looking for Stark. All of them not knowing what he looks like apart from an old prison picture that shows him as a kid still wet behind the ears.'

He dug a pipe out of his jacket pocket and began to tamp tobacco into it. Essex marched back and forth in front of him, the worry lines seeming to deepen by the moment.

'Stark ripped off the pick-up truck, but he ain't gonna be stupid enough to stick with it for long. So he'll ditch it and crawl into a hole while he tries to make contact with Groves. Everyone knows what Groves looks like. So all we gotta do is get a line on Groves and wait for him to go to Stark or Stark to come to him.'

'I still don't like it.'

'Who the hell does?' Gorman snapped, then struck a match to set fire to the tobacco. He laughed and the sound was a taunt. 'But I guess it's natural you like it least of anybody. Because you goddamn know it's gonna break you, you goddamn fairy.'

Essex seemed about to explode into a shrill-voiced temper again, but the bleep of the telephone froze the rage on his face. Then he lunged towards the instrument. Gorman scooped up the handset.

'Yeah?'

'That's not Rick!' A man's voice with just a trace of camp. Gorman recognised the speaker.

'It goddamn ain't, Charlie.' Charles Swenson ran the Trans-Canadian Escort Agency office in Toronto. Essex had stopped making time with him when Danny Walker came on the scene and svelte, good-looking Charlie had been trying to get back into the top man's bed ever since.

'Oh, Mr. Gorman.' He couldn't quite manage to keep the distaste out of his voice. 'Is Rick there?'

'He's where I can get a message to him,' Gorman answered, grinning at the angry Essex.

'Oh. Well, I guess you ought to know about it, too, Mr. Gorman. Groves is in his office here in the city. Somebody saw his Caddy parked outside the building. We got a man with night glasses into a place across the street. Groves seems to be trying to get some sleep at his desk.'

Gorman's hawkish face showed a broader grin – of satisfaction rather than in reaction to Essex's chagrin. 'Terrific, Charlie.'

'Ask Rick if he wants me to come up to the duplex will you, Mr. Gorman?'

The vice-president in charge of Ontario covered the mouthpiece with a big hand. 'Dan Groves is camped in his Adelaide Street office. Waiting to hear from Stark, looks like. Or maybe waiting for him to turn up. Charlie Swenson wants to know if you'd like to party.'

Essex breathed a sigh of relief. Gorman's plan looked like paying off. A man like Groves who could afford to buy the Royal York Hotel and not miss the price, wouldn't elect to sleep in the discomfort of an office chair without good reason. The Canadian company's top executive felt sufficiently unburdened of anxiety to ignore Gorman's tone.

'Tell him I'd like to see him up here, Harry.'

Gorman uncovered the mouthpiece. 'What cover have we got on Groves?' His tone was even, businesslike, crisp.

'Delorn himself and three of his men watching the building, Mr. Gorman. And somebody from technical is trying to find out if it's possible to gimmick communications.'

Delorn was the top enforcer in Toronto. The company's technical branch was precisely what its title implied. One of its members was attempting to tap Groves' telephone.

'So it's nicely wrapped up for the night, Charlie. Rick says to get your ass over here, if you know what I mean.'

Swenson didn't know how to respond and Gorman saved him the trouble by hanging up. Then he heaved himself out of the chair and stretched.

'You'll take charge?' Essex asked.

'Goddamn right,' Gorman replied.

'Finish it fast, Harry. We've got Spagnoli coming to Reindeer Mountain tomorrow. We don't want any trouble while he's around.'

'Don't wet your frilly pants, Rick,' Gorman said lightly as he moved towards the door. 'Soon as Stark makes contact with Groves that British bastard will be dead. Have a ball with Charlie and then go meet the Yank. With peace of mind, Rick. About Stark, anyway. See you around.'

Gorman let himself out of the plush apartment and Essex stared malevolently at the closed door. Then he whirled towards the drinks cabinet, but shook his head angrily. More and more lately, as Gorman flexed his muscles and dropped veiled threats about assuming the presidency of the Canadian arm, Essex had resorted to liquor as a calming influence for his nerves. That wasn't good. Scotch ruined his concentration, and dulled his performance in bed.

So he confined himself to pacing the room, allying it with chewing on his nails, as he waited for Swenson to arrive. Charlie was as good as Danny in the sack: even a little more inventive. But he was lacking in another talent which Danny had in full measure. Charlie was not a cold-blooded killer. However, maybe . . .

There was a discreet knock on the door.

Stark slept soundly in the comfortable bed of room one-o-seven in the Windsor Manor Hotel. Physically he was completely at rest, his bruised and battered body recovering by degrees. But his mind hovered just below the level of awareness, attuned to spring into alertness at the slightest sign of danger. It so happened it was immaterial that his stiffened muscles would be slow to respond to the dictates of his agile mind. For the company was seeking to reach him through Groves, of course. So no check had been run on Toronto hotels with the object of pin-pointing new guests with British accents.

A few blocks north of Front Street, Dan Groves was also sleeping. But less soundly, sprawled uncomfortably across the desk in the tenth floor office of the building which bore his name. The blotter beneath his cheek was spotted with the now dry tears he had shed for Belinda Jarratt. Grief for the dead girl and regret that he had taken the decision which resulted in the tragedy had sprung the tears and kept them flowing until the ducts were empty and exhaustion overtook him.

From the tenth floor office of a real estate broker immediately across Adelaide Street from the Groves Industries Building, Lew Delorn watched the sleeping man through powerful night-glasses. Harry Gorman relaxed in the rich comfort of a leather swivel chair behind a mahogany desk. Once the telephone rang. Gorman answered it with a grunt and was told there was no way to put a tap on the switchboard through which Groves' line ran. Also, Danny Walker's pick-up had been found.

Below, an enforcer sat at the wheel of an Opel Rekord parked half a block down from where Groves' Cadillac Brougham crouched at the kerb. Two other enforcers, huddled deep in their upturned coat collars to combat the chill of the Toronto night air, blew on their cupped hands as they watched the side and rear doorways of the Groves Industries Building.

Across town in the south east, Rick Essex lay in euphoric exhaustion across the quilt covering the circular bed in the duplex. The quilt was of black silk and the man's white flesh made an obscene contrast. He was naked and replete with sexual satisfaction. His shrivelled genitals were swamped by the sag of his hairless belly.

'Was I better than Danny, Rick?'

Essex raised his head wearily and smiled towards the door which gave on to the bathroom. Charlie stood there, posed provocatively. He was also naked. Tall and slender with well-developed muscles encased in hard flesh. Blond hair brushing his shoulders. Dyed, of course, for the broad patch on his chest and that which covered his legs and became thick and bushy at his crotch was a sheened black. He was twenty-seven and still retained the bloom of youth in his green-eyed face which was girlishly pretty. He was the kind of homosexual who was blatantly proud of the fact.

'You always were,' Essex replied tenderly. 'Come and kiss me.'

The younger man advanced on the bed and knelt down beside it, craning forward to lower his face towards that of his partner. He had satisfied Essex without reaching his own climax and his want was powerfully obvious as he crushed down with his lips and probed with his tongue. Essex could taste the faintly sweet tang of the mouthwash Swenson had used.

'Will it be me for always now?' the younger man asked hoarsely as he tore their lips apart.

'It was only Danny for a special reason,' Essex whispered, and rolled over on to his bulging belly, patting the bed.

Swenson stretched out beside him. 'I'm ready to do anything you want me to, Rick. Anything he could have done.' His delicate-looking but strong hands explored Essex's smooth back, moving downwards.

'Anything, Charlie?'

Swenson's fingers kneaded the flesh more frenetically and hooked a foot over the older man's ankle to draw his legs into a wide vee. 'You know, Rick,' he whispered, and his hands clawed, his fingers sinking into flesh.

'Even kill Gorman?'

Swenson smiled wickedly as he rolled into the triangle of the splayed thighs. 'I've been longing for the day when you'd ask me.' His sigh was of dual ecstacy.

CHAPTER SEVEN

THE Faversham Hotel was a dump. A cheap flophouse on Queens Quay at the waterfront. The noise of the harbour assaulted it from the front. Traffic on the Fred Gardiner Expressway streamed past the rear. And just beyond the main cross-town road, trains rattled and whistled their way back and forth along the tracks of the CN and CP railroads.

But Stark had not gone there for peace and quiet. The Faversham was the rendezvous point chosen by Groves who, if he followed Stark's instructions, would not arrive for another thirty minutes. It was eight o'clock when Stark turned off the street to mount the four steps leading up to the shabby entrance of the hotel. He had walked there from the Windsor Manor, needing the exercise to loosen his muscles rested by sleep and eased by a long soak in hot, soapy water.

'Help you?'

The gloomy lobby of the Faversham smelled of stale sweat, fresh urine and dead flies. It felt colder than the morning air outside. The man behind the scarred desk was about sixty and looked tired enough to have been awake the past ten years. He had bloodshot eyes and the stink of gin on his breath. But he knew class when he saw it and probably guessed the exact high price of the clothes Stark was wearing.

'Top floor room. Just for the day.'

The old man also placed the British accent. He had little else to do in life except study the characters of his guests.

'Gotta charge you the rate for a day and a night. Six-fifty. In advance, on account of you ain't got no luggage.'

Stark gave him a ten dollar bill stolen from one of the enforcers at Lake Riding Lodge. He signed the register swung towards him, using the name Frank Welles. The old man did not ask to see his passport.

'Can't make change this early in the day.'

'Don't expect you to, mate,' Stark told him. 'What I do expect is a man. He'll be here in less than thirty minutes. Send him straight up to whatever room you're giving me.'

The old man took a key from a bank of pigeon holes. 'Number twenty. Ain't much, but then we ain't got much.' He crouched low to read the name Stark had signed. 'I'll make sure your visitor finds you, Mr. Welles.'

There was no elevator and Stark's banged-up right knee was protesting painfully by the time he reached the top, sixth floor of the hotel. To Stark, who viewed every confined space as a potential trap, the upper floors of buildings were normally to be avoided. But one of the reasons he had told Groves to delay his arrival was to give himself the opportunity to case the hotel.

Ignoring the closed door of room twenty, he climbed a final flight of stairs, pushed open a hinged panel in the landing ceiling and stepped out on to the roof. Already the morning smog was rising from the waking city, bringing the horizons closer. But he had not come on to the hotel's flat roof to admire the Toronto skyline or watch the St. Lawrence Seaway and Great Lakes shipping cluttering the harbour. He ignored the western side of the roof and concentrated on the front and the eastern side. From the front, in the cover of the disused neon sign proclaiming the name of the hotel, he had a clear view down into Queens Quay. And an examination of the side convinced him he could make the jump from the Faversham to the roof of the office building next door. Six floors was a vertigo-inducing distance down. But the alley was no more than eight feet wide. It was not an easy jump and his injured knee gave off a sharp stab of pain in anticipation. But, if his survival depended upon this escape route, he was convinced he could make it.

He angled back across the rooftop and squatted behind the *S* of the sign again. The telephone call to Groves at seven o'clock had been short and to the point.

'This is me. Where?'

Groves had answered half a second after the connection was made. He sounded tenser than a virgin bride on her wedding night. 'Faversham Hotel, Queens Quay. Do you know how—'

'I'll find it. Be there at eight-thirty. Ask at the desk for Frank Welles' room. You'll be followed. Don't worry about it. Don't try to lose them.'

'Followed? But I—'

Stark had hung up, dialled room service and asked for breakfast. He ate it while he was soaking in the bath. Then he had started out to walk to the hotel after asking at the desk for directions to Queens Quay. He hadn't known the Faversham was a cheap doss for society's dregs and a trick drum for streetwalkers. Groves did, so he left the Cadillac and arrived by cab. With his suit crumpled from having slept in it and his face stubbled, he looked like a more likely guest than Stark.

The man on the roof spared only a glance for the man transferring from the taxi to the hotel. Then he raked his low-lidded blue eyes in both directions along the street. He saw the cream coloured Opel Rekord angle into the kerb half a block behind the cab and park. He watched the four beefy men climb out. Two of them moved into the side street west of the hotel. One stayed at the foot of the cracked steps and lit a cigarette. One entered the hotel a minute after Groves had gone in. Stark spent another minute and a half watching the streets for signs of reinforcements. He saw no likely-looking muscle and backed away to the trapdoor. He cracked it open just as Groves was rapping his knuckles on the door of room twenty.

'I preferred the penthouse, mate,' Stark called.

The delay between hearing from the Revenger and seeing him had produced nothing to calm Groves' nerves. The man started so hard he seemed to leap off the floor. He no longer looked dignified and the change owed little to the crumpled clothing. Mostly it was the dark stubble on his jaw and the haunted look in his grey eyes, the whites of which were as red-veined as those of the old man on the reception desk. He seemed not to trust himself to speak and he stumbled as he mounted the stairs. He was panting.

Stark left the trapdoor and went to each edge of the roof. The enforcer who had entered the hotel was outside again, talking to the man by the steps. This man went to the side and the rear to round up the other two. Then all three hurried to the front entrance. Groves was out on the roof by then. Stark lowered the trapdoor, but there was no way to fasten it from the outside. And nothing heavy enough to rest on it and keep it shut.

'Belinda? How did she die?'

Out in the bright sunlight penetrating the air pollution, Groves looked older and more badly used than he had in the gloom of the landing.

'An easy way,' Stark told him. 'I wouldn't think you feel a thing when you're blown to bits. Forget her. Four company enforcers are coming up the stairs right now. After they find we're not in room twenty, no telling how long it'll take them to check the roof. Has the company got the gall to knock off a VIP like you?'

Grief for Belinda constricted his throat for a moment, but he recovered quickly. 'I'm no use to them dead.'

'Fine, because you'd never make the long jump,' Stark answered, eyeing the gap between the roofs. Then he shook off the doubt that he might not be able to cover the distance himself. 'Fill me in fast.'

'I've got a son,' Groves said, abiding by the instruction for speed. 'His name is Bill. He's twenty-five and mixed up with something called the Trans-Canadian Escort Service. That's a company operation.' He looked as if he was going to be physically sick and had to swallow hard to hold in the nausea. 'It deals in prostitution. Male prostitution. Supplying good looking young men to rich old women.'

They were standing ten feet away from the trapdoor, Groves following Stark's cue and keeping his voice low. It was close enough for both of them to hear the heavy footfalls of the quartet of enforcers on the sixth floor landing.

'The details don't matter. Just tell me who you want killed and point me in the right direction.'

Knuckles rapped on a door panel below. 'House detective, open up!' a voice growled.

'I don't know where he is,' Groves said, looking at the trapdoor with frightened eyes. 'You'll have to find him through Trans-Canadian. But there's an agency office in every provincial capital and some other cities.'

'For what you're paying I didn't expect it to be as easy as looking in the telephone book,' Stark acknowledged as a hint of apology entered Groves' haunted eyes. 'But you do know his name?'

Groves started to look sick again. Below them, there had been another two demands for the door of room twenty to be opened. A woman had yelled for some quiet so she could sleep. A boot or a shoulder hit the door and it crashed back against the inner wall. But Groves' misery had nothing to do with this.

'Bill Groves. My son.'

Stark received the news without emotion. 'I only make judgements on company men, mate. And they're always guilty. If your boy is on the payroll, killing him won't give me any bad dreams.'

'Check every room in the bloody place!' a man snarled, and footfalls thudded against the uncarpeted floor and stairway. Not the flight up to the roof – yet.

'When it's done, you'll find me at the Capitan house. Capitan's a town in Alberta, a few miles north of Edmonton. You can reach me by telephone at Capitan double five zero one.'

There was more shouting below. Arguments. Between men and men and men and women.

'Anything you want, anywhere you want it, phone me at that number. I'll arrange delivery. It'll take me until this evening to get home.'

'Probably take me a little longer than that to get a fix on

the target,' Stark said wryly. 'Just one thing for now. In any connection, do you know a man named Essex?'

Beyond the identities of the three enforcers he had killed at Lake Riding Lodge, plus the existence of a male prostitution circuit which Groves had just mentioned, the name Essex was all he knew about the Canadian arm of the company. A name which had come to his blast-punished ears while he was crouched on the beam in the stable barn, listening to the three enforcers approaching across the debris-littered yard.

Footfalls sounded on the flight of stairs leading up to the trapdoor. Not fast. Tentative.

'There's Rick Essex, of course,' Groves said, too intrigued by Stark's question to be aware that the meeting would shortly be forced to an end.

'Why of course?' Stark asked, delving a hand into his right jacket pocket and half turning to face the trapdoor squarely.

'He's a big man in Canada. Into all the leisure and recreational industries. A theatre chain. Bowling alleys. Ski resorts in the north. Marinas on the lakes. We're fellow members on the committee of a charity foundation. Are you saying that Rick Essex is mixed—'

'Like Belinda, forget him,' Stark cut in.

He didn't want a gun battle on the rooftops, unless it was inevitable. He had got what he wanted from Groves and staying around purely for the pleasure of killing a few easily replaceable enforcers wasn't worth the police heat such an act was sure to generate.

'I'll be in touch,' he said, whirled and launched into a run.

Groves shouted something after him, but Stark didn't hear what it was. Neither did Lew Delorn. He simply heard a voice which told him someone was on the roof. And this triggered a fast response. He went up the final few steps at a run, drawing a Colt Commander from a shoulder holster. He tucked his head down and smashed the top of his back against the trapdoor. It crashed open and thudded against the roof.

Stark took off from the unguarded edge of the hotel roof, fighting the impulse to look down the tapering perspective into the alley. He had to gain height as well as length, for the roof of the office building did offer token protection for the unwary: by means of a two feet high coping. He also had to pump his legs, so that the good one which had powered his lunge from the hotel took the major impact of the landing on the office building. He made it – just. His left foot found the top of the coping, shoe heel slamming into the angle. But his body was erect and as he sought to get a foothold with his trailing leg he could have toppled backwards. But he leaned forward and flailed his arms, pitching himself painfully at full stretch against the tarmac surface.

The sound of the trapdoor crashing open masked his groan of pain, and urged him into movement – wriggling and rolling to lie parallel with and pressed against the coping. He dragged the revolver from his pocket.

'Where the frigging hell did he go, Groves?' Delorn snarled. Then he peered back down the stairway. 'Up on the roof, you guys!' he yelled.

Groves stood in a sagging posture, his shoulders slumped and his head hanging as he stared down at his shoes. But after a fast glance around the roof, Delorn didn't need verbal or any other kind of information from the man. It was obvious Stark could have taken only one escape route.

'Beat it, you stupid bastard!' he rasped. 'And wait for the price to go up.'

He knew Stark had made the leap across the alley. And he could see that the only cover on the roof of the building next door was the elevator motor housing. There was a closed inspection hatch this side. Perhaps a way down into the building beyond. Groves was slow to respond to the order that he should leave. He only started towards the open trapdoor as Delorn made his decision and started the run.

He kept the big automatic in his hand in case his decision was the wrong one. It was, but the gun didn't help him.

Delorn was big and he was athletic. The leap was well within his capabilities and he made only one mistake. His eyes and gun were directed towards the shell over the elevator motor. If Stark was waiting, that was where he expected him to be hiding. But, as Delorn landed two-footed and well-balanced on the coping, Stark sprang up immediately in front of him. Delorn tried to bring the gun down to the aim. Stark chopped hard at his wrist with his forearm. His head butted the enforcer in the groin. Delorn, his face contorted into a mask of terror, toppled backwards. The Colt Commander dropped from his clawed hand as he sought to grab hold of Stark. He missed. His shoes lost contact with the coping and the scream became piercingly shriller. He kicked and flailed, his body tumbling downwards in corkscrewing cartwheels. He didn't touch the walls which echoed his high-pitched anguish. He hit the concrete head-first. His skull shattered and the no-longer rigidly held flesh squashed and burst. His body and limbs smacked into the pulpy stain and crumpled. The snapping of bones was like the sound of static electricity crackling.

Stark didn't hear it. He hadn't stayed at the roof's edge long enough to see the start of Delorn's death fall. In dodging the grasping hand of the doomed man, he had stooped, snatched up the fallen automatic then whirled to sprint for the hatchway into the elevator motor housing. Like Delorn, he had been unable to see if there was another way into the building beyond. And he had no time to check – in case there wasn't. For the other enforcers were almost on the hotel roof. He could hear at least two of them, their voices growing louder as Delorn's scream faded, telling Groves to get out of their way. He didn't know whether Groves was acting with a predetermined purpose or not. It wasn't important. All that mattered was that his attempt to get down the stairway was hampering the progress of the enforcers trying to reach the roof.

The door opened smoothly, and Stark closed it silently. Enough light filtered through a dirt-grimed frosted window on the far side for him to see the lay-out. A centrally located electric motor supported over the shaft by iron girders. A grilled catwalk all around. Ample room for a man to slide between the edge of the catwalk and the motor. But only if the car was at the top of the shaft. Looking down, Stark saw four lengths of plaited wire cable descending into an infinity of blackness. Then the motor whirled. The drums played out the cable, lowering the car.

He turned, and found a crack in the door. The angle of vision it offered was not panoramic, but wide enough. The motor sighed into silence. He was able to see three men spring up through the trapdoor opening. They advanced cautiously towards the edge of the hotel roof, each thrusting a gun out in front of him. The motor started again – winding in the cables. Only now did Stark become aware of the strong smell of oil in the confined space. It reminded him, unaccountably in such a situation as this, of one of his first jobs after leaving the south London grammar school. Tea-boy and general dogsbody in a Bermondsey garage where he learned the practicalities of motor car engines before he was old enough to drive the cars.

One of the enforcers didn't like heights. He held back, looking everywhere but down, while the others surveyed the shattered body at the centre of the massive bloodstain six floors below. The motor stopped. All three men stared hard across the gap. The smashed-up remains of Lew Delorn warned against the leap. Then they spun around, thrusting the guns into holsters, and ran towards the trapdoor opening. Stark turned away from the crack and looked down at the roof of the elevator car. It was just visible, two floors down. Too far to drop on to in free fall. He eyed the cables, black with thick grease. It would be a slide rather than a climb. The impact would be hard and the grease might not prevent agonising friction. He thought about the enforcers racing down through the hotel to cut off his escape. Then he began to take off his jacket to protect his hands. The motor restarted. The cables wound in around the drum. The car slid up past the doors of the fifth floor without stopping.

Stark shrugged back into his jacket and dropped into a sitting position on the catwalk. When the car halted at the head of the shaft its roof was only eighteen inches below his feet. He lowered himself silently on to the thick carpet of grease and dust. The doors hissed open and he thought he heard just the one passenger enter. He looked for a hatchway under the filthy layer and found it. He knew he didn't have the time to ride up and down on the car waiting for it to be empty. As the doors closed and the motor whined into the descent cycle, he pulled open the hatch cover. It wasn't hinged – simply lifted out.

He looked down on a girl of about sixteen whose prettiness was marred by adolescent acne. But she had nice legs. She was showing the whole length of one – she thought for her own eyes only as she surveyed its reflection in the mirrored rear wall of the car, readjusting the twisted tights. She was not aware of Stark until he dropped down through the hatch, favouring his injured knee. Then she squealed and let the hem of her dress fall.

'Don't mind me, darling,' he said with a grin, leaning nonchalantly against the side wall. 'You carry on.'

Her shocked gaze travelled up towards the hole in the roof and returned to Stark's face. 'Where did you come from?' she gasped.

The car dropped below the fourth and third floors without stopping.

'Up above,' Stark told her. 'But don't worry, sweetheart. Flashing your legs isn't a mortal sin and I won't report you.'

She was carrying a manilla file. The car halted at the second floor. When the doors slid open no one was waiting to come in. The girl continued to stare at him.

'Your floor?' he asked.

She shook her head, but it wasn't a negative gesture. She

was just clearing it. Then she scuttled out of the car. 'You're crazy, man!' she yelled hoarsely.

'Remember to say your prayers tonight!' he answered through the closing door.

Seeing his finger on the button, he became aware of the grease and dust on his hands from opening the hatchway. He thrust both hands in his pockets. The car stopped and he sauntered out into the empty lobby. The street outside was empty of pedestrians for half a block in both directions. Everyone was crowded into the alley, pushing and shoving for a closer view of the shattered body. A police siren wailed, rising in volume as the law came nearer. He elbowed his way into the crush of eager rubbernecks. People yelled at him, but he was deep in the midst of the crowd when the three enforcers rushed breathlessly down the crumbling steps at the entrance of the Faversham Hotel.

'I'm a doctor!' Stark told a tough-looking stevedore ready to throw a punch at him for getting an elbow in his ribs. He endeavoured to conceal his English accent with a mid-Atlantic drawl.

'Doctor!' the man yelled. 'There's a doctor coming! Let him through there!'

A corridor was opened up through the crowd. Stark moved down it, nodding curtly in response to people who gave him room to pass. He reached the open space around the bloodied heap of human flesh with points of fractured bones sticking up through ripped clothing. Nobody was prepared to venture forward on to the massive splash of crimson. Even Stark stayed close to the hotel wall to avoid getting blood on his shoes. There were only a few sightseers in this section of the alley. Two teenage boys, a matronly woman and an elderly couple. They, like the people on the other side of the body, looked at Stark anxiously. Stark had been eyeing the body pensively as he moved around it in a half-circle. Now he rubbed a hand over his jaw. It was clenched into a fist to hide the dirt and he used the back of the hand.

'It is my considered opinion that the man is dead,' he said

solemnly. 'In which case there is nothing medical science can do to help him. Good morning.'

He pushed through the small knot of people and sauntered along the empty stretch of alley. It took several seconds for the shocked crowd to find its collective voice. And then it was not to shout at him to stop. Merely a communal mumbling with a scornful tone. As he emerged on to a narrow street, a panting man ran towards him.

'Hey, it it right a guy took a dive off a building around here, mac?' he asked with gasping excitement.

'I heard a guy's been putting it around he's an angel,' Stark replied, maintaining the drawl in his voice. 'Maybe it was him and he tried to fly.'

CHAPTER EIGHT

RICK ESSEX was feeling good as he hovered in the twilight world between sleep and waking. The heavy drape curtains were drawn across the bedroom windows, keeping out the nine o'clock sunshine of the new day. And the only sound was the hiss of the shower water needling on to the hardness of Charlie's exquisite body. Essex sought to remain in this pleasant state of semi-limbo by conjuring up a dreamlike image of the naked young man in the shower. But then the strident bleep of the telephone shattered the illusion and Essex was thrust into irritable alertness. Then, as he reached for the handset of the instrument on the curved bedhead shelf, he recalled what Charlie had promised to do for him.

Abruptly, his mood changed for the better. Allowing the telephone to bleep some more, he took the time to press the button which electrically swept open the drapes to shaft hazy sunlight across the bedroom. Harry Gorman was going to die and he was going to be killed by somebody Essex trusted implicity. On cue, Charlie appeared in the bathroom doorway, soapy and dripping wet.

'Oh, I was going to get it.'

'You dry yourself and get us some breakfast, sweetie,' Essex told him. 'Then perhaps there'll be time to seal our bargain before you drive me out to the airport.' He hooked the handset to his head. 'Rick Essex, here.'

'The bastard got away!' Gorman snarled. No preliminary snide remarks about Essex and Swenson. Straight down to business, talking in an angry tone that was perhaps a screen for fear.

'What happened?' Essex's mood underwent another rapid change as he was assaulted by a bad case of jitters of his own.

'Not on the 'phone!' Gorman shot back. 'We had him and we lost him. We also lost Lew Delorn. For good.'

'Law?'

'Picking up the pieces, but no heat on the company. You want to put out the word coast-to-coast now?'

'Do it,' Essex instructed, and smiled. 'All reports to come to me at Reindeer Mountain. I'll be there tonight.' He pulled rank by toughening his tone. 'And that includes a report from you on what went wrong, Harry!'

He broke the connection and broadened his grin. Although he was as anxious as any company executive to see Stark taken out, Essex could draw a lot of comfort from Gorman's call. The big, tough-talking sonofabitch had made his first boob since being promoted from enforcer to vice-president in the company's well-defined careers structure. Maybe that didn't cancel out the grave error of judgement Essex had made in the first attempt to get Stark: but at least it would serve to keep Gorman in line until Charlie shut his mouth permanently.

'Good news, Rick?' Swenson asked as he brought in a tray loaded with coffee, juice and cereal for two.

'It could have been a lot worse,' Essex replied as Swenson sat on the side of the bed and carefully smoothed out a place to set down the tray. He told him what Gorman had reported.

'Doesn't that mean you have a solid reason for taking out Gorman now?' the handsome young man asked, a little sullenly.

Essex reached out a hand to pat him gently on the cheek. 'It does, sweetie, but I don't intend to go through official channels to the international board.'

Anybody on the company payroll below executive status could be taken out at the discretion of the local top man. But permission to eliminate an executive had to be obtained from Rome.

Swenson smiled and pressed his face hard against Essex's hand. 'Then I can still do you the favour?'

'You sure can, and I trust you to do it.'

'I love you for that, Rick.'

'And I love you for not attaching any strings.'

'We're not all Danny Walkers!' Swenson muttered with a contemptuous toss of his head and a tone of bitchiness.

During a quiet interlude last night, Essex had told his bedmate about the deal with Walker. The coldly calculating bisexual enforcer had agreed to accept the top-secret assignment to kill Gorman, but there was a condition. When Walker wasn't allowing himself to be balled by men, he was indulging in two more expensive pastimes – playing the tables at Las Vegas and making it with straight, high society women. Both were luxuries that cost more than he could ordinarily earn as an enforcer. And he was strongly attracted to the quarter of a million dollar bonus that was on offer to whoever took out John Stark.

So the deal had been struck: Walker was to be given first crack at Stark whenever the Revenger reached Canada. And it was a solid bet that the blood-lusting Britisher was going to cross the Atlantic, providing a European arm of the company didn't take him out first. For the Canadian arm had good reason to keep tabs on Dan Groves, and the multi-millionaire industrialist was currently on an extended visit to Europe, constantly showing up in each country where Stark made his presence violently felt. A hard enough probability for Essex to stake his future security as president of the Canadian arm of the company on it. Probability had become fact when Groves flew from Stockholm to Montreal, sans Belinda Jarratt who had been close to him throughout the European stay. A cryptic telephone call over the under-ocean cable link had provided Essex with the information that the Jarratt woman was en route for Toronto in the company of a young man. A fast local check on Groves Industries gained him the details of the plan to have a chauffeured limousine meet the airliner winging in from Stockholm via New York.

All the enquiries had been made discreetly, so that just Essex had been aware of the possible identity of Belinda Jarratt's travelling companion. Essex, and then Danny

Walker plus the other enforcer and the technical branch man he selected to help him. Two men who would doubtless have been taken out immediately the job was completed: for a third of a quarter of a million would have been two-thirds less than Walker was prepared to accept.

After they had finished breakfast there was just time for a double-header before Essex had to shower, shave and dress for the ride out to the airport. Swenson drove him in his salmon pink British Lotus Elan. There was no privacy for an intimate farewell so the two men merely shook hands before Essex went through the gate to board the Trans-Canadian flight for Edmonton. Swenson went up on to the observation platform to watch the seven-o-seven make a safe take-off, then hurried back to the Lotus in the short-stay car park. He took the Spanish-made flick-knife from the glove compartment and transferred it to a side pocket of his pale blue sports jacket before setting the car rolling. He used the car telephone to call the escort agency office, telling his deputy he would probably not be in until midday. His deputy reported that there were no problems.

Swenson had one – locating Harry Gorman, who might be anywhere in Toronto; anywhere even in the whole province of Ontario since Stark was free and on the prowl in the vice-president's territory. And it was important that Swenson find him quickly, so that he could take him out while Stark was still handy to be blamed for the killing.

He used the mobile telephone several more times as he cruised towards Toronto on the road from the airport – checking the obvious places. Gorman's home in Swansea south of the city. The Dundas Street office of Essex Leisure Limited from where Gorman controlled all company operations in the province. His city apartment on University Avenue. His wife didn't know where he was, his office was as keen to find him as was Swenson and there was no reply on the apartment number.

After drawing these blanks, the handsome homosexual with dyed blond hair and murder in his mind was happier than if he had got a positive reply. For it was obvious Harry Gorman had gone to ground to lick his wounds after the failure to get Stark. And Swenson happened to know where Gorman went when he needed consolation. Forsaking company fun girls, he used the services of a independent prostitute who operated from a cheap three-room apartment above a barber's shop behind the *Toronto Daily Star* building. Swenson happened to know this because he had been taking a particular interest in Gorman's habits and movements since the enmity between the province vice-president and the national president had become apparent to such a careful observer as himself.

He left the car on a parking lot off University Avenue and strolled casually along Pearl Street, to all intents and purposes a man out enjoying the warm spring sunshine. The barber's shop was busy, but he didn't have to pass through it to gain access to the apartment above. A hallway at the side led to a stairway which rose to a short landing blocked at the end by a door. Swenson's gait could be as silent as it was graceful and he made no sound reaching the door. It was his skill as a cat burglar which had led to his recruitment by the company – and the soon-to-follow intimate friendship with Rick Essex which gained him fast promotion to executive running the Toronto escort agency.

Silently, using the stiff clear plastic holder in which he kept his driver's licence, he tripped the lock on the door. He eased it open slowly for he had no idea of the apartment's layout. Silence oozed out through the crack. Then a voice. A woman's murmuring. Too low for Swenson to hear what she was saying. He knew her name was Norma Fouchet and that she was a prostitute who drew most of her clients from the customers of the barber's shop below. He knew nothing else about her. Yet he intended to kill her. The mere fact that she was a woman was enough to make that no hardship.

He slid into a tiny hallway and eased the door closed behind him. Two other doors were open. One showed a cramped kitchen with dirty dishes in the sink and cobwebs on the ceiling. Swenson wrinkled his nose. He hated untidiness. The living room through the other doorway was little better. It was small and overcrowded with unmatched furniture that was burned by cigarettes and otherwise marked by ill-use. The painted walls bore the stains of carelessly opened beer bottles. Norma Fouchet was not in the champagne end of the market. Ashtrays overflowed, magazines littered the floor and the atmosphere was pervaded by the citric odour of orange peel. The woman stopped talking and began to laugh. Swenson crossed the room on tiptoe and squatted in front of a closed door. He put his eye to the keyhole and felt physically sick. Sometimes the mere thought of heterosexual coupling aroused nausea in his throat. Actually seeing such an act made the bile more bitter. He was able to see the entire length of the bed from his vantage point. Gorman was completely naked, and under different circumstances Swenson might have been excited by the sight of his powerful, well-proportioned body. But not now. For the man was arched over the willing woman who was not quite nude: she wore thigh-length black leather boots and vivid red rubber kitchen gloves. Her booted legs eased wider and wider as the man sank down towards her. Then her gloved hands groped to guide him. Her garishly painted mouth gaped wide as the laughter gave way to the panting of forced passion. Her slightly convex stomach trembled and her thighs, creamy white between the black tops of the boots and the dark tangle of the pubic hair, quivered.

Then, an instant before the woman could stab his rigid member into her gaping sex, Gorman froze his sinking motion. Swenson poised himself to whirl and run, fearful the man had sensed an intruder. But it was just a new twist in the commercial sex play.

'Suck, not fuck, baby!' Gorman groaned.

Norma Fouchet had played the part before. As Gorman moved his body one way on the bed, she slid in the other. The man had bought the woman and felt he owed her nothing more – in money or anything else. His belly smothered her face, his thigh ground into her breasts and Swenson knew he must have sunk into her throat. What the man crouched at the keyhole didn't know was the reason why Gorman was craning his neck to look up. For he could not see the two strategically placed wall mirrors: nor the lower half of the woman's body. Gorman was watching Norma Fouchet's rubber gloved hands as they worked agilely on her own body.

Swenson stopped watching. The bitterness in his throat and the wet feeling in his stomach combined to make him feel giddy. But he shook free of the sensation and glided silently across the room to the door of the bathroom. At one time the apartment had not been fitted with such a luxury. But then a corner of the living room had been partitioned off. Not much of it: just enough so that a toilet bowl, a hand basin and a shower cubicle could be installed. The shower curtain was on nylon runners and Swenson pulled it across in front of him with a soft swishing sound. A gasp from Gorman and then a bout of harsh coughing from the woman told him when the sex act was completed. He took out the knife and buttoned out the four-inch blade with a soft click. The pleasure of anticipating what was to come blanketed his mind to the former distaste.

He didn't care which of his potential victims came to him first: and never even considered the dangerous but unlikely possibility they would visit the bathroom together. The bedroom door was wrenched open. It was the woman, her coughs giving way to gags. She ran into the bathroom, Gorman's laughter following her. She closed the door and leaned against it for a moment, breathing deeply through her nose, her homely face in its frame of dishevelled black hair expressing passive resignation to her suffering. Such mistreatment was a hazard of her profession. So was murder, but she hardly ever thought of this. She had not time as the acknowledged danger became a brutal fact.

As she bent over the hand basin and turned on both faucets, Swenson opened the shower curtain. The gushing of the water covered the sound of the runners. His soft soled shoes made no noise against the tile flooring. She had her gloved hands cupped under the cold faucet and was sucking the water into her punished throat when the knife struck her. Its assault was an underarm one, Swenson's hand swinging below her arched body. The blade entered her flesh just below her left breast and was so angled that it penetrated deep into her heart. There was an instant of a dying scream but all it produced were a few air bubbles bursting on the rising water level. For with his free hand, Swenson had plunged Norma Fouchet's face hard into the basin. A spasm jerked her dead body and he stepped away from her, withdrew the knife and released his grip. Even before she became inert after crumpling to the floor, Swenson had wiped one of his hands down his pants leg. The hand which had been soiled by touching a woman. Then, once again, distaste was masked. This time by the sheer pleasure of staring down upon the corpse. A pleasure increased because the body was that of a despicable female. A hint of scorn made the smile even more evil. To think Rick had considered him incapable of murder. Christ, the blood-dripping flick-knife had claimed the lives of more women than the Boston strangler.

'Hey, you gonna stay in there all day?'

The harsh voice of Gorman, loud enough to reveal he had left the bedroom for the living room, jerked Swenson out of his mood of self-indulgence. Slipping the blade into the woman was just the added excitement of the trimming. Harry Gorman was the real package, destined to pay for every wisecrack and insult he had directed at Swenson. That was the beauty of the deal with Rick. It wasn't really a favour to him at all, killing Gorman. For Swenson had his own reasons for taking out the straight sonofabitch. But that the murder would get him in more solidly with Rick . . . that was beautiful.

The hand basin was overflowing. Swenson reached through the curtain and turned on the shower. He had to touch the woman again, to lift and tumble her body into the cubicle.

He got his jacket only slightly wet. The overflowed water diluted the woman's blood to a faint trace of pink. He was just in time to flatten himself against the wall, behind the door as Gorman thrust it open. The big man was still naked.

'You're the most careless, messiest dame I've ever —'

Gorman had held still in the doorway for part of a second, gazing at the water cascading over the sides of the hand basin, hearing its splashing and the hiss of the shower. Then he went forward, arms outstretched to turn off the faucets, yelling at the woman as he moved. It was Swenson's reflection, in the mirror on the wall above the basin, which curtailed his shouted words. He saw the handsome young blond emerging from behind the door, but failed to spot the knife. He felt it as he started to whirl: stabbing into his lower back to one side of his spine – searing deep through skin, tissue and veins to penetrate the left located kidney. The wound was not instantly fatal. But it was crippling. Gorman's whirling motion slowed, then stopped as Swenson withdrew the knife. A great gout of blood arced from the wound and splashed into the overflow, immediately losing its crimson vividness. Gorman's only sound of pain was a grunt. Then his legs gave way and he sat down hard, splashing the pink tinted water.

'Essex didn't have time to put it through Rome,' he gasped, bringing his hand around from his back and staring incredulously at the blood on his fingers. Then his pained eyes swung their gaze up at Swenson.

'Just Rick and me, you sonofabitch!' the good-looking fag answered. 'And we're the only two people who'll ever know it wasn't Stark who took you out.'

The pain was getting harder to bear, but Gorman was not just a tough talker. He had come up the hard way, often getting as much as he was able to give. 'Stark'll take care of Essex. He specialises in the top boys. And you, you cock-sucking bastard – you'll get yours.'

The life was draining out of him with the blood and his anger was pumping the crimson flow at a fast rate. He sagged weakly to lean against the wall. This put his head under the cascade of water spilling from the basin. But he was beyond reviving. His breathing was ragged and the lids sank to mask his no longer sharp eyes. The evil smile sprang across Swenson's handsome face again, and he was galvanised into rapid action. He went forward a pace, stooped, and slashed his knife hand down and across. Every remaining ounce of Gorman's diminishing energy powered a scream. It emerged as little more than a squeak. His eyes had drawn wide and they stayed that way when he died. Their final sight was of a length of his shrivelled flesh floating away from his groin, trailing blood into the water on which it was carried.

Swenson moderated his actions to a casual haste, dipping the knife blade in the water, wiping it on a towel, then pivoting and going out of the bathroom. His shoes squelched from the sopping wet that had impregnated them. He found the whore's purse and delved for a lipstick. Using it as a pencil, he printed a message in large block capitals on the living room wall: IT WAS NOT KILROY – JOHN STARK WAS HERE. Then he squelched down the stairway, turned right on Pearl and strolled back to University Avenue. His shoes felt uncomfortable, but he left no footprints after the first few steps. He drove up the avenue to his apartment near the university to change, wondering how long it would take the water to seep down into the barber's shop. He wondered, too, if Stark would still be in Toronto when news of the double killing attributed to him broke in the media.

But Stark was long gone, at the wheel of an Avis rented Chevrolet sedan, covering the same stretch of highway along which he and Belinda had been chauffeured yesterday. After walking well clear of the Faversham Hotel, he had hailed a cab to return to the Windsor Manor at the other end of the category scale. The hotel had changed his traveller's cheques into hard cash and he used some of the money to pay the bill. It was just a short walk along Front Street to Union

Station. But, as he surveyed the destination board, he decided against taking a train. From Toronto, anyway. The railroads out of the city were too easy to cover: whether the tracks south towards the border with the United States or the two main lines starting north then swinging east for Ottawa and west for Sudbury. And the company would surely cover them. The police, too, if they got a lead to his involvement in the Faversham Hotel incident, perhaps through a calculated leak by the company. Flying had the same disadvantage. Likewise the long distance buses of Colonial Coach, Gray Coach and the Greyhound line. Stealing a car was dangerous initially, fairly safe in the short term then became progressively more risky. He didn't look like a hitch-hiker and central Alberta was too far to walk!

So he went into an Avis Rental Agency and used Danny Walker's driver's licence from the dead man's billfold to buy the use of the dark blue, late model Chevrolet. And he was several miles out on the freeway towards Barrie when Charlie Swenson left the bed of Rick Essex to take his shower. When the blond young man was waiting in a more utilitarium bathroom to commit double murder, Stark was barrelling the sedan along Parry Sound to the French River stretch of the Trans-Canada Highway. His ultimate destination was Capitan and the house of Dan Groves.

The fact that here was the last place the company would expect him to be was no part of his reason for going there. Since telling Groves during the short, sharp meeting on the hotel roof that he didn't need to know the details behind the assignment to kill, he had decided the opposite was true. Groves' rueful comment: *I'm no use to them dead*, and the no-sweat way in which the enforcers had allowed him to leave needed explaining. Also needed was proof of Groves' intention to give him cover when the assignment was completed. So far, all Stark had received was a free, safe trip to Canada, a passport that may or may not be of use again in the future and a thousand dollars. Which was more than he needed to indulge in his self-elected vocation of attacking the company and the men who ran it whenever and wherever he had the opportunity. But to be given a particular target – especially such an intriguing one – Stark wanted to be sure of payment in full. And he wanted it in advance. Because Canada was a big country and he could find Bill Groves in the furtherest-flung corner of it: in circumstances which did not allow him the time to wait around for delivery of Groves senior's promises.

And if none of this worked out? Then a small-fry male prostitute working the company's vice circuit would probably continue to give his father problems – unless he happened to get in Stark's way. For the Revenger had a more important target in mind. His name was Essex, unwittingly fingered by the enforcer at the Lake Riding Lodge. Whether this was the same Richard Essex Groves had told him about, he couldn't be sure yet. But a chain of leisure interests was the perfect front for the company. If that should turn out to be a dud, however? If Essex was just the head of the local enforcers, only worth the trouble of taking out should he happen to step in front of a gunsight? Then Stark would find a way to the big boys of the Canadian arm through the escort agency. Branches in every major city, so why stay around Toronto with the heat turned on? Best to go in cold on new territory.

But it wasn't as easy as that. It never was. Night had fallen with a shower of rain that fast developed into a torrential downpour. It happened beyond Sault Ste. Marie where the waters of Lake Huron and Lake Superior meet in a narrow neck to form the border between Canada and the United States. The weather was fine and the light good when he drove through the city. The Chevvy's trip meter had clocked a lot of miles, but he felt only slightly weary. Then, with the lashing rain and the dark of night, the strain of the long drive caught up with him.

It was on a stretch of highway running between the lake and the foothills of Batchawana Mountain. The country was as wild as the weather and there was no sign that a town would show up for another thousand miles. He had the wipers switched to high speed but still the billowing curtain of rain beat them for most of the time, forcing him to keep his speed to a crawl. Even then he had to lean forward over the wheel, peering through the shape-distorting waves of water smashing against the curved glass.

The posture saved his life. For the bullet that shattered the windscreen burrowed into the seat backrest instead of his chest. But he knew it could be nothing more than a reprieve. He stomped hard on the accelerator and punched a hole in the abruptly opaque milkiness of the safety glass.

'Don't you ever fucking well give up!' he yelled above the throaty roar of the racing engine.

CHAPTER NINE

THE Essex Bar of the Reindeer Mountain Country Club was discreetly lit at night. In contrast to the day time. For then the entire building swung around in a slow arc, the sliding glass panels which formed one wall constantly in line with the sun from the time it rose until it set. If it was an overcast day, the bar rotated through part of a circle anyway for its timing mechanism was set a year ahead to take account of daily changes in sun ups and sun downs. It had not been cheap to install such complex machinery, but then expense was no object at the country club.

In addition to the Essex Bar, it comprised many other features for the amusement of its high-paying exclusive membership. An eighteen-hole golf course, an outdoor swimming pool filled with sea water, an indoor one which was heated, six tennis courts – three grass and three hard – two restaurants, four static bars, a nightclub, a theatre and a bowling alley. Because of its remote location in the north of Alberta some fifty miles west of Wood Buffalo National Park, the club also had extensive living accommodation. This was provided by two English-style manor houses and thirty log cabins. The whole complex was spread over a broken plateau south of the three thousand foot high Reindeer Mountain. Access was by private road which spurred off the main highway up to Hay River on Great Slave Lake, or light aircraft from Edmonton to a landing strip at the foot of the mountain and helicopter to the plateau fifteen hundred feet above sea level.

Rick Essex had used the latter method to complete his trip from Toronto but he did not fly in the Aerostar 601 utilised for guest transportation. Instead, he piloted his own Cessna Citation twin-engined jet which had been flown in for him from Vancouver.

Entering the bar which bore his name, which formed a part of Essex Leisure Limited's most extensive and profitable enterprise in the coast-to-coast chain of recreational facilities, the Canadian arm's top man felt good. The scheduled flight from Toronto had been a bore. But in Edmonton there had been nothing but good news. As he arrived at the downtown local office of the Trans-Canadian Escort Agency, a call came in from Toronto. He took it in private in the manager's office, but Charlie Swenson spoke only two words.

'It's done.' Then he hung up.

Angelo Spagnoli flew in from Los Angeles two hours later, right on time. During that period, Essex looked over the local operation and discovered for himself that the executive in charge of Alberta province had told no lies in his monthly reports. Company business was running smoothly and profitably on all its many fronts.

The visiting fireman from the American West Coast syndicate operation proved to be a quiet, middle-aged man very eager to be impressed by what Essex had to show him. A little too meticulous, perhaps, but none of his questions was asked without good reason and it was obvious all the answers he received were carefully stored in his memory. Fortunately, he had come to look over only one facet of the evil which existed behind the ultra-respective front of Trans-Canadian. For the organisation he represented was longer and deeper into conventional large-scale crime than was the more recently established company. What he had come to examine in detail was the Canadian arm's specialty – the supply, on a high mark-up basis, of virile and handsome young men to add excitement to the barren daily (and nightly) lives of sagging, time-eroded old women. Rich women. It was the company's male prostitution ring which interested Spagnoli.

Essex was able to endure the boredom of explaining the basic principles of the operation, and the tedious business of going over the accounting figures, simply because the Italian-

American was such a personable and interested student. And Spagnoli's attitude and responses appealed to Essex's ego. For everything which was good about the operation – and nothing was revealed to be bad – the visitor heaped praise upon Essex personally.

Then came the jet flight up to Reindeer Mountain to show Spagnoli the theory put into practice. And since Essex regarded piloting an aircraft as a game of skill – pitting his abilities against the capabilities of the machine and the vagaries of nature – it was one of the greatest pleasures in his life.

To round off the day, upon which the presence of Stark in Canada was the one blot (and he chose to push this problem into the back of his mind), a final gratification awaited him. Spagnoli was comfortably located in one of the luxuriously furnished cabins, to take a bath and a nap before viewing the Reindeer Mountain set up. And this gave Essex ample time to do what he must.

Soft music floated through the dimly-lit, perfume-heavy air of the Essex Bar as he tramped across the deep-pile carpet. The clink of ice in glasses added a counterpoint, the combination providing a pleasing cover for the many low-voiced conversations emanating from the many booths which jutted out along three walls of the large room. Heavy drape curtains were drawn across several of the booths for the light level was not discreet enough for the purposes of some couples. Nobody occupied the less private tables in the central open area of the room and the row of stools strung out along the front of the hammered copper bar were empty. A half-dozen waiters, all husky young men dressed in tight pants and tunics opened to show their hirsute chests, criss-crossed the room, responding to the numbered light signals which flashed on a panel behind the bar. They greeted Essex deferentially by name.

'Good evening, Mr. Essex,' the head bartender said softly as Essex climbed on to a stool. 'Pleasure to see you at Reindeer again.'

'Pleasure to be here, Sonny,' the honoured guest replied, nodding his thanks as a bottle of Haig Pinch and a shot glass were set before him. And he meant it. The handsome young men in their tight uniforms were at the country club to indulge the fantasies of the aging female, fee-paying guests. But there was nothing in the rules to say Essex could not enjoy looking at them. He had a different kind of fantasy and a less conventional method of bringing it to reality, that was all.

'Bill Groves been in tonight?' Essex asked after he had poured a drink and sipped at it. With everything going so well, he could drink for pleasure rather than support. 'They tell me over at the Western Manor House he and Mrs. Thorncroft left their suite an hour ago.'

Sonny was one of the few employees at the country club who had spotted Essex as a homosexual on the tenet that it takes one to know one. He always endeavoured to be solicitous towards the top man but had yet to discover Essex made it a rule not to mess with the hired help below executive status. 'I saw him earlier, Mr. Essex. I'll check.' He moved along the bar to the point where the waiters collected their ordered drinks, and had to speak to three of them before he got what he wanted. 'Booth nineteen, Mr. Essex,' he reported.

Essex nodded and shot a glance over his shoulder. The drapes of the specified booth were not drawn. He finished his drink, slid off the stool and strolled across the room. The couple were seated close together on the leather-covered bench on one side of the table. The fact that the drapes were not drawn was an oversight. Bill Groves had a hand down the low cut bodice of Mrs. Thorncroft's dress, fondling one of her enormous breasts. One of her hands stroked his face while the other was occupied beneath the table top. His drink was untouched while her glass was empty. But it was not entirely alcohol that put the glitter into her eyes.

'Oh, I'm sorry,' Essex said. 'The curtains were open.'

Hands were abruptly withdrawn. Groves – twenty-two,

tall, dark and handsome – was embarrassed. Mrs. Thorncroft, a sixty-year-old divorcee who was grossly overweight, had a bad skin and dripped with jewellery, simply looked annoyed.

'There's an urgent call for Bill,' Essex explained in a soothing tone. 'I think he should take it, Mrs. Thorncroft. If you could spare him for a while?'

The fat, ugly old woman sighed out of her annoyance. It was her first visit to Reindeer Mountain. Fully aware of its exclusiveness, she didn't want to spoil her chances of a return by causing trouble. 'You won't keep him long?' There was something obscene about the look of yearning she directed at Groves.

The man crept both his hands beneath the table and his zipper made a hissing sound.

'You won't be bored,' Essex assured, and turned to crook a finger towards one of the waiters not engaged with an order.

The youngster hurried over, matting of chest hair glistening in the soft lighting, tightly encased hips swaying rhythmically.

'Bill isn't the jealous type, Mrs. Thorncroft,' Essex said with his most charming smile, which was usually reserved for men. 'He won't mind Roy standing in for him – providing you approve.'

The woman's predatory eyes surveyed the slender young boy and became hungry as they settled their gaze upon the bulge at his crotch. Then her false teeth were exposed in a grin which made her look like a horse laughing. 'I approve most wholeheartedly.'

Roy smiled, successfully hiding his revulsion for the repulsive old woman. The pay for waiting at tables in the Essex Bar was good. But all those rocks sparkling from the depth of the booth gave promise of a tip that could double his take home salary this month.

Embarrassment gone, Groves was nervously curious as he slid from the booth seat and Roy took his place. Mrs. Thorncroft immediately pressed the button to draw the drapes.

But that only needed the one hand. Her other had delved below the table to test the evidence of her eyes even before the curtains had closed to mask the booth.

'A call, Mr. Essex?' Groves asked as he fell in beside the shorter man, heading for the exit from the bar.

'An excuse, Bill,' Essex told him, and winked. 'I guess you're not too broken-up about being prised loose from that man-eater?'

Groves immediately felt better. It was worrying to be summoned by the top man personally. And the talk of an urgent telephone call hadn't exactly had a calming influence on his jolted nerves. But now, as Essex smiled benignly while they walked down the stone steps to where a vivid yellow jeep was parked, Groves' mood lightened.

'I reckon she's the worst one yet, sir.'

'But generous with it?' Essex asked with a grin as he got behind the wheel.

Groves sank on to the passenger seat. 'Only this afternoon she called a Calgary dealer and ordered a Mustang, sir.'

'I won't ask what you had to do for that.' He started the engine.

Groves shuddered. 'Don't!'

The company got its profit from the fees paid by the women to the agency, and the bills which were run up at Reindeer Mountain and other, less well-endowed, Essex Leisure recreational centres spread throughout the country. Any gifts, in money or kind, given to their young companions were entitled to be freely retained. The men were paid a salary, plus commission when they steered their rich clients on to company preserves.

Essex invited no further conversation during the mile drive over a winding track to his personal cabin in a grove of pine trees. The northern night air was cold and it was an open jeep, so both men welcomed the centrally-heated comfort of the cabin, which was more isolated than most within the boundaries of the country club complex. Essex continued to play the old pals act after they had entered, settling

Groves in a deep armchair and giving him coffee instead of liquor when he expressed his preference. The top man poured a double shot of his favourite brand of Scotch for himself. But he didn't drink it. Instead, he held the crystal glass between the palms of his hands to keep from chewing his nails as he paced up and down in front of Groves.

The younger man, his relief at being released from his duties towards Mrs. Thorncroft becoming a dim memory, grew progressively uneasy again as he watched Essex's silent pacing.

'You were a good pupil up at Snowy Ridge, Bill,' the top man said at last to break the long pause. 'You did the course in record time and there hasn't been a single complaint about you since you went on the Calgary agency's list.'

Essex was neither smiling nor stern. His deeply scored features were set in a neutral expression. But Groves didn't like the way the man refused to meet his quizzical gaze.

'I've always done my best, sir.'

Essex nodded his agreement. 'I know that, Bill. Everyone knows it. But sometimes a person can get into a bind not of his own making.'

'A bind, sir?'

Now Essex looked at him and showed a flicker of a smile. 'Drink your coffee. It'll all work out, but I've decided you ought to be put in the picture. It's your father. He's causing us some trouble.'

Groves' strongly handsome face which showed a marked family resemblance to that of his father, became tight-lipped and hard-eyed with rising anger.

Essex shook his head. 'Don't blow your top, Bill,' he said quickly. 'I didn't spring this interview on you with the intention of getting you uptight. You joined us because you hated your old man but had the taste for his life style. You walked out on all that easy money he was giving you and started to work for the hard bread. Not nice work, but the pay's been high. Higher than the average – and not because you're one of Trans-Canadian's most accommodating escorts.'

'I know that, Mr. Essex,' Groves said tensely.

'Okay, Bill,' Essex urged. 'Just drink your coffee and listen to what I'm saying.'

Groves nodded and sipped from the bone china cup. Essex continued with his pacing.

'You laid it on the line for us, Bill. You came to us and told us you wanted to get back at your father any and every way you could. And we agreed to help you – not out of charity, as you well know. It served both our interests when you posed for the pictures and we took them. You were launched on a highly rewarding career and at the same time put your old man on the rack. We had the lever we needed to get into the most lucrative sections of Groves Industries Incorporated. It was a good two-way deal.'

Groves wanted to say something. Essex had stopped pacing and was looking at him expectantly, waiting to hear his comment. But, try as he might, the younger man could only open and close his lips: no words would come out. For a moment he blamed the struggle to hold his rage inside him on the constriction in his throat. But then the paralysis abruptly spread to draw the strength from his limbs. The cup and saucer slipped from his limp hands and fell to the carpet without shattering. The coffee stain didn't look too serious against the dark coloured patterning.

Essex was smiling at him as he raised his stare from the stain to look at the man. The benign, almost avuncular smile. 'One of the amphetamine group of narcotics, Bill,' he explained in the same quiet, even tones as before. 'Not fatal in the dosage I gave you. Just sufficient to relax you if you don't fight it.'

Groves tried to fight it. But it could only be a mental struggle. His body remained helplessly slumped in the chair, supported by the arms and backrest. The front of his pants showed a spreading dampness as he lost control of the voluntary physical functions. Essex resumed his pacing.

'But when you make a deal with the company, Bill, it only remains in force for as long as it continues to serve our business purposes. Naturally, that was not explained to you at the outset of our relationship. I am only telling you all this now because I feel it is right a man should know the reason why he is going to die.'

All Groves' organs continued to function normally. His heart beat and his lungs pumped. He retained the use of his senses, his brain and his mind, except that the nerves controlling speech and muscular movement were frozen. Thus, he could experience terror but produce no overt reaction to it. This and the utter helplessness of the man magnified his anguish beyond measure.

'You are going to die because your father has brought John Stark to Canada. If you know about Stark and his mission, all well and good. If you don't, I will merely say that your father could have chosen no surer way to antagonise me and my organisation. So much so that I am prepared to forego the opportunity you have represented. To release the lever on Groves Industries Incorporated. Simply for the satisfaction of paying back your old man.'

He stopped, immediately in front of the paralysed man, and swung to face him. He swallowed the large drink at a gulp.

'And you should applaud my decision, Bill.' He grinned. 'Because your death will cause him more agony than anything that's gone before. For you know as well as I do that despite what you feel for him, your old man loves you. It's a parental quirk I find difficult to understand, but it is undoubtedly a fact. So, rest in peace, Bill. You've achieved your ambition beyond your hopes.'

Essex set down his glass on a low table, then carefully picked up the cup and saucer and put these out of harm's way. Groves' unuttered screams were resounded and amplified within the terrified confines of his head. His muscles would not respond as he tried to press himself deeper into the chair. He thought the clawed hands were reaching out to close on his throat and strangle him. But instead they fastened over his shoulders and tipped him forward, head-first out of the chair. He smelt himself and the spilled coffee. Essex stooped, clasped his limp wrists and moved in an ungainly, crouched, reverse walk. Groves was dragged, face down, across the carpet of the living room, through a doorway and then over the smooth tiles of the kitchen floor. There, he was allowed to remain in helpless inertia for a few moments.

Essex did not switch on the fluorescent tube lighting, but a soft glow from the living room floor lamps fell through the open doorway. Groves was able to watch Essex with just one eye, peering across his numb forearm. His tormentor was squatting close to the hob set into a run of laminate worktops. He had positioned himself sideways on, purposely so that his victim could witness his actions. Below the hob was an oven and as Essex swung open the door, Groves snapped his eyes closed. He tried to summon every ounce of energy from the still functioning parts of his body and channel it into voicing a scream. He refused to acknowledge that the cabin was too remote for rescue to be feasible.

It didn't matter anyway. The gentle, even voice of Rick Essex told him that the piercingly shrill plea for help which threatened to puncture his own eardrums was trapped inside his head.

'These microwave ovens have got a built-in safety factor so you can't switch them on with the door open. Protects from accidental burns. But this won't be any accident, of course. And I didn't get to be top man in the company by letting problems phase me.'

He used a knife from the cutlery drawer in a unit beside the hob, unscrewing a plate at the bottom of the oven. As top man it was not, of course, necessary for him to do his own killing. Despite Bill Groves' family connections, he was still merely another professional gigolo expendable because he was replaceable. But Essex had started out on his company career as a killer. Not the enforcer type, confined to a specific territory. A target man with the whole of Canada his beat, his services utilised when somebody important needed to be taken out. Working quietly and discreetly; taking his time, choosing his weapon, his method and his scene. Then moving in, doing his job and getting out. There had never been a slip up and the Canadian arm of the company still was trying to recruit a target man who could come somewhere near to approaching Essex's coldly calculated skill.

The problem of the oven was easy to solve. With the base-plate removed, he was able to wedge the knife handle against the safety cut-out and thus keep the circuit open despite the yawning door. Then he straightened up and clicked the control knob to full heat. A red indicator light glowed. It was the only sign that the killing microwaves were now streaming through the inky blackness of the oven. He switched off the current.

'I guess you've been stewing for long enough,' he said lightly. 'Time to see how you bake.'

He laughed harshly.

Groves attempted to induce unconsciousness but the narcotisation of that section of his nervous system controlling his physical being had the effect of heightening his mental sensibilities. The more he tried to dull his brain into a trance, the greater became his awareness to vivid reality.

Essex picked him half off the floor by grasping him under the armpits this time. As he turned and dragged him, his arms trailed out at his sides. His shoulders would not fit into the oven while he was strictly prone. So Essex tilted him, wedging him inside at an angle. He shoved him far enough in so that the top of his head rested against the back wall of the oven.

'You leave this world knowing you've made some dear old ladies very happy, Bill,' Essex said, and clicked the control knob to full.

Groves experienced a split-second of excruciating agony. Then he was dead. Perhaps the sensation was of burning, but it didn't last long enough to define. The microwaves hit him and penetrated through him. In an instant the molecular structure of the brain matter, bone and tissue of his head was thrown into violent confusion. Countless million infinitesimal particles raced in a thousand different directions, creating enough friction to cook his head in its own liquid. The mere displacement of the natural order of things killed his brain instantaneously. It took a further fifteen seconds for Essex to be convinced that the involuntary spasm of the limp body had signalled death. For although his murders had always been quick and clean in the actual committing of the act, he had never used this method before. Microwave ovens had not been around in his younger days.

He switched off the current and grabbed hold of Groves' ankles to drag his head and shoulders from the oven. The dead man's face was hot to the touch, but looked in no way different from before. He left the body on the kitchen floor while he removed the knife and refixed the baseplate in position. Then he went into the living room, pleased he did not feel the need of a drink. It meant he had not lost his touch. The armchair was still warm from where Groves had been slumped in it. He picked up the telephone, feeling an ache in the pit of his stomach. He recognised what this was and held off his local call to make a long distance one.

'Charles Swenson?' The handsome young blond sounded tired, as if the call had roused him from sleep.

'Rick, sweetie. How about joining me at Snowy Ridge tomorrow?'

The man in Toronto was abruptly wide awake. 'First flight I can get booked on.'

Essex broke the connection and dialled the internal number for the reception office. 'Get the truck up to my cabin,' he instructed. 'Call the Yank and tell him I'll pick him up in ten minutes. And get a message to the Thorncroft dame. Tell her there's been a death in Bill Groves' family. Very sudden. He had to go. It'll be a long trip.'

He cradled the handset and sighed. His day was complete – for no word had yet reached the Reindeer Mountain Country Club about what had happened in the shadow of another mountain a thousand miles to the south-east.

CHAPTER TEN

THE road curved sharply to the left but Stark didn't see it. Through the jagged hole punched in the opaque windscreen he could see only the lashing rain shimmering in the headlights. And this through narrowed lids almost closed against the spiteful beat of the drops sucked into the car and hurled at his face. The wipers continued to sweep back and forth, one of the arms passing over the gaping hole like a finger waved in a chastising gesture.

But he knew he was off the road as soon as the smooth ride ended. The car canted, front end down, as it plunged on to a slope. The man with the rifle was over to the right somewhere. The angle of the bullet's entry into the car had shown that. Another bullet was fired. He didn't hear the shot above the roar of the engine, lash of the rain and the harsh curses ripping from his lips. But he heard the clunk as lead penetrated metal. Somewhere in the Chevvy's rear end.

He stomped on the brake pedal. The same gunman or another? Maybe there were a dozen of them crouched in the rain. In a group or spread all around? Right at that moment it didn't matter. What was important was that the speeding car was off the paved surface: plunging ahead. And he couldn't see what the hell was in front of him. Except the wedge of the headlights reflected against slanting rain and dazzling him. It was a situation that spelled suicide and he chose to try to evade that and take a chance on being murdered.

All four wheels locked and he had no way of knowing if that was good or bad. All he could do was hang on to the wheel, keep his right foot hard on the brake pedal and wait. No. One other thing. He killed the lights. If he didn't know where the hell he was going, he sure wasn't going to make it any easier for anybody else to see where he finished up.

The car turned sideways on to the decline of the slope. He could smell the fresh scent of grass crushed by the sliding tyres. The front end tried to swing around to pirouette the Chevvy in the opposite direction. But then the slope ended. The wing crumpled against a rock that refused to move. The back end slammed down on to level ground. The car tipped, teetered, and rolled. Stark flashed a hand away from the steering wheel for long enough to turn off the ignition. There was a brief space of time when just the beating of rain against metal disturbed the silence. While Stark hung upside down in his seat belt's grip. Then the weight of the engine crunched the front end into a dip. The rock which had tipped the car now drove a deep dent into the bonnet. *They call it a hood out here*, he thought. The car rolled on to its side and he smacked hard against the door. Then it crashed down on to its wheels, tried to tip again and couldn't make it.

All Stark's old injuries resurrected their former pains and some new ones started to throb. But the future was more important than the present. He hit the release button on the safety harness, sprang open the door and dived out of the car. Torrential rain soaked him instantly and three bullets clanged into the Chevvy's body shell. He powered into a roll through long, sopping grass: cursing. Himself, rather than the gunman, for overlooking the interior light. As the door opened, it clicked on to provide his ambushers with a marker beacon.

Without the roar of the big engine beating in his ears, he heard the rifle reports. But he was unable to pinpoint the men's position yet. The grass became suddenly wetter and less springy. He halted the roll and realised it was not grass any more. But reeds growing at the shallow edge of a stream. He jerked the Colt Commander from the wet, clinging pocket of his jacket and peered around, trying to get his bearings. In the teeming rain it wasn't easy. But it was a little better once the giddiness of the roll had passed and his eyes readjusted from staring so long at the wedge of light beamed from the Chevvy's headlights.

The stream curved away behind him, swollen and muddy, running fast towards Lake Superior hidden beyond a swathe of timber. Ahead of him, across a grass strip of wide stream banking was the crippled car, the front half of its bonnet gaping open as if to emit a silent scream and its door hanging wide like a broken wing. Beyond the car, the incline started, and finished at the edge of the curving road. Above this, the jagged ridge of mountain tops showed solid black against the marginally lighter shade of the swirling rain clouds.

Four men were outlined in menacing silhouettes at the edge of the road. They just stood there, peering down at the car and beyond it into the reeds where Stark was concealed. The range was about two hundred feet and if Stark had a rifle the men would have been like clearly defined targets in a shooting gallery. But he had only the Colt Commander and the little S.&W. ·38 revolver. They had the rifles, swinging them gently back and forth, covering the general area where they knew Stark to be.

They were company enforcers from Sault Ste. Marie, sent out with two others even before Stark reached the city of the massive Soo Locks. No company man was indispensable. Executives were harder to replace than those of a lower order, but they all had deputies constantly ready to assume responsibilities when their superiors were unable to continue. Thus it was in the case of Harry Gorman, when the leakage of water into the barber's shop on Pearl Street in Toronto led to the realisation that he would never again be responsible for anything.

Because neither the whore nor the barber had any company connections, it was the Toronto Police Department which took the squeal on the double killing. The company heard of it through a reporter on the police beat, and a man was immediately available to step into Gorman's shoes. And with Stark's name scrawled on the wall of the prostitute's apartment, the top priority was obvious. Get the Revenger before he could do any more damage.

Back-tracking on what Gorman had learned from Essex

about Stark's arrival in Canada with Belinda Jarratt, they were able to discover from airport contacts that Stark had a passport in the name of Frank Welles. A blanket search of the city revealed he had stayed at the Windsor Manor Hotel but checked out shortly after the Faversham Hotel incident and before Gorman and the whore were murdered. While the city search continued, a check was made on public and private transportation out of the city in every direction – even via Lake Ontario. Posing as a city detective, the company man who examined the Avis rental records spotted the name Danny Walker and knew he had struck pay dirt. John Stark, alias Frank Welles, had killed Danny Walker. The addition was easy and the total was money in the bank. A description and the licence number of the rented Chevrolet sedan was communicated to every company executive throughout the provinces of Ontario and Quebec. By car, Stark could not have made it any further. With just his real name to work on, the Toronto police were non-starters in the contest to locate the wanted man. And with a quarter of a million dollars prize money due to the winner it was a contest every company man – and woman – was eager to enter.

In fact, it was an informer in a bar in the small town of Blind River who made the first sighting of Stark. He saw the Chevvy angled nose-in to the kerb outside, and then spotted Stark at a table, finishing a sandwich and coffee. He used the bar himself, to make a call, after Stark had left. He called a number in Sault Ste. Marie because the Chevvy had barrelled off in that direction and there was nowhere else in between.

There was no Trans-Canadian Escort Agency in the city. A travel organisation specialising in boat tours of the lakes acted as a front. The executive in charge arranged for Stark to be tagged and followed into town. But, in the event the Revenger did not make a stop-over, he despatched six enforcers in two cars out along the highway north of the city. This stretch of the Trans-Canada Highway is one of the most desolate and under-used main roads in southern

Canada and offered a thousand places for an ambush before it reached Wawa, a hundred and fifty miles away.

Stark made no stop-over, and so the six men sent out ahead of him were able to launch their attack. The idea had been to kill him at the wheel, or at least disable him so that he plunged the car off the road: either down the slope into the rushing stream or into the solid rock of the escarpment on the other side.

But the bastard's luck had continued to hold good. He was down there now, somewhere in the long grass and tall reeds between the wrecked Chevvy and the stream. And they were not going to look for him until they had some light. So they merely waited for it to arrive, tensed to retreat should Stark begin throwing lead at them: or to blast at him with their 7·62 mm Schultz and Larsen rifles if he showed himself.

He didn't reveal his position, and even when the two cars were brought from their hiding place around the curve of the road, their headlights illuminated only the wildly flowing stream and the wrecked Chevvy. One of the two cars which rolled off the road and parked with powerful beams spraying down the slope was an old Ford Torino. The second was a brand new British-built Range Rover, designed for rough cross-country travelling. This had a movable spotlight on the driver's side of the windscreen and when the head beams failed to show the quarry, the spot was swivelled from side to side, raking the rain-streaked darkness with a wedge of light.

'We're gonna have to move in on the bastard!' one of the enforcers growled tensely.

'Maybe he crawled outta the auto and died,' another suggested hopefully.

'That's called wishful thinking, Rand.'

'Could have wound up in the river and drowned.'

'So? We still gotta find his body. Ain't gonna be no bonus paid just because we say we think Stark's dead.'

The enforcers organised their advance, using the four-wheel drive, multi-geared British vehicle. One man to drive, another in the passenger seat with the window rolled down and rifle slanted through and two on foot behind, using the bulk of the Range Rover for cover. The other two men remained crouched behind the dazzling beams of the Ford's headlights.

The Range Rover inched over the lip of the slope and started down, heavy-duty tyres maintaining traction on the sopping wet grass. The spotlight wavered from side to side, a pointing finger probing the night with bright menace. But there was a limit to the arc it could sweep and by the time the big car was halfway down the slope, Stark was beyond the range of its scanning exploration.

He was stretched full length in the reeds a hundred feet upstream from where his roll had ended. Still trying to recover his breath after fighting the strong flood current on all fours while the men on the slope were waiting for the cars to come. The rain and the soaking grass had made his clothes like sodden rags and started his flesh shivering. The stream water was colder, but he was beyond the point where mere chill and wet could increase his wretched discomfort. But bullets ripping into him would certainly raise the level of pain he was feeling from the car wreck: if he lived long enough to experience it.

He had to stay where he was until the Range Rover reached the obstacles of the rock and the crippled Chevvy. If the driver elected to swing to the right to go around, his lights would sweep over Stark's hiding place. He did go right, but immediately straightened again. Stark moved, slithering along on his belly and propelling himself with elbows and the toes of his shoes. He held the automatic in one hand and the revolver in the other. The reeds swished and water squelched beneath him. But the rush of the stream, the hiss of the rain and the low growl of the Range Rover's power unit provided more than enough noise to cover these slight sounds.

Then he was in the grass, which was long enough to hide him as far as the foot of the slope. But on the upgrade it grew less tall. He began to doubt if he had put enough distance between himself and the enforcers. But it was too late to worry about that now. The Range Rover had halted and the men had split into two pairs. One couple started downstream and the other headed in Stark's direction. Stark had no time to lose. For two reasons. The immediate one was that six company men were stalking him here and now. In addition to this, he had to consider reinforcements. He had no idea where this half dozen had come from, but they had certainly launched their attack from ahead of him. Even the company did not have ESP. He had been spotted back down the road. So it was a pound to a penny they would be coming at him from that direction soon and had held back to avoid alerting him to a tail.

He ran up the slope, body crouched and head ducked into the rain: angling away from where the Ford was parked. The sound he made did not worry him. Only if an enforcer happened to see his moving form against the grassy backdrop would he be revealed. And that could happen just as well if he crawled. The slope curved, following the course of the road and within a few moments there was a hump of solid ground between the hunted and his hunters. He reached the top, and slowed his pace. He walked across the hard shoulder and over the tarmac. On the opposite side of the road, he angled right. Keeping close to the escarpment, he moved back towards a point opposite where the twin splashes of red marked the position of the Ford. He didn't see the two men standing near it until he had recrossed the road. Both stood to the right of the car, peering down the slope, rifles held in a two-handed grip with fingers around the triggers. Carried at hip level, but poised to thud up to the shoulder.

Stark moved forward on the balls of his feet, guns thrust out in front of him. The concentration of both enforcers was focussed on the bank of the stream. But Stark had first-hand knowledge of how the presence of an enemy can be sensed before he is physically seen. And he knew how a man's nerves, when he is in a tense situation, can cause him to glance in every direction at the dictates of a fear-ridden imagination. But these two were over-conscientious in their duty of providing cover for the men below. Their imaginations were dormant and if they had a sixth sense for danger, they had no time to react to it.

Stark halted three feet behind them, pressed a gun muzzle against the nape of each neck and squeezed the triggers. The double report merged into a single crack. There were no screams because both men lost their voice boxes as the bullets smashed through their necks and exited from their throats. A dying nerve in a finger squeezed a trigger. A heavy calibre bullet hissed through the rain and cut into the white water of the rushing stream. Blood gushed from the throat wounds and the enforcers followed the crimson sprays to the ground.

The men below were still within the fringe glow from the Ford's headlights: inching forward, their rifles raking the ground ahead of them. But, as the closely spaced gunshots sounded, all four pitched into the grass.

'What the hell, Rand?' one of them yelled. 'Where is he?'

One of the dead men had collapsed on to his rifle. Stark thrust the handguns into his pockets and scooped up the accessible rifle. He knew that both the bodies and he were invisible from below, screened by the dazzling lights of the car. Despite the sound of water, falling from the low sky and rushing between the stream banks, Stark did not even attempt to imitate a Canadian accent. Instead, he ripped open the Ford's door and slid behind the wheel. The keys were in the ignition. The transmission was manual. The rifle across his lap, door still open, he slammed the gears into reverse, started the engine and released the parking brake. At least two, maybe four, bullets were exploded towards the car as it charged backwards. He slammed on the brakes, and left the engine running. The car was angled across the centre of the road, protected from further shots by the lip of the slope. He switched off lights before lunging out of the car. Before he could be silhouetted against the craggy rock of the mountainside, he pitched to the ground. He bellied forwards, hearing the Range Rover's engine cranked into raucous life. The bodies of the two dead enforcers humped the top of the slope. Stark rested the rifle across one of them. The other stared at him in mute enmity with dead eyes.

'You blokes started it,' Stark muttered with soft vehemence.

None of the men below was going to be caught in the open. All knew Stark had not high-tailed it away in the Ford. The lights had been turned out instead of arcing around to show the way ahead of the speeding car. And the engine note had changed from high revs to an even idle. All had raced for the Range Rover, the first man to reach it climbing behind the wheel. The others piled in through the passenger door as the engine fired.

Stark saw the big, ungainly-looking car as it lurched forward and was swung into a tight turn to face towards the slope. There was nothing ungainly about the way it moved across the water-logged ground. Its big tyres cut deep ruts in the turf, but every square centimetre of carved rubber which made contact with the ground produced traction. It raced up the slope, spraying water and hurling up clods of dirt.

When the car was within fifty feet of him, Stark shattered the windscreen. Just to make it difficult for the driver. He didn't expect to hit anybody. There was no time for any fancy shots at the headlights or tyres. He lunged upright and sprinted to the left. The big car continued to plough a water-spraying course up the slope. The driver had stuck his head out of the window to see where he was going.

Stark pulled up short and pivoted, throwing himself down at the ground again: facing the car. He fired as it crested the top of the slope. He saw blood gush from the hole in the crown of the driver's skull. Then he cursed. The dead man was flung back into the car by the impact of the bullet. His foot stayed hard against the accelerator pedal, but the steering was set free. The offside front wheel bumped over one of the dead men on the ground and the front wheels were fractionally swivelled from centre alignment. The Range Rover roared towards the Ford. More curses ripped from Stark's lips as he waited to see his escape vehicle wrecked.

But a man inside the bigger car saw the impending crash and lunged at the steering wheel. Another man kicked the dead driver's foot off the pedal. The Range Rover arced across the front of the Ford with a crunch of bumpers coming together. The Ford leapt backwards a few inches. The Range Rover slowed. But not enough. And the man who had a one-handed grip on the steering wheel was not able to get sufficient lock.

The car was travelling at about twenty miles an hour when it piled into the escarpment. It impacted with its offside front corner. The bumper on the rugged vehicle was not just a piece of trim put on for style. It absorbed the crash solidly. The car stopped dead. The man in the front passenger seat was pitched through the already shattered windscreen, slid along the bonnet and smashed open his head against the mountain rock.

Stark couldn't tell about the others until he had approached the stalled car, moving cautiously through the teeming rain, finger curled and exerting first pressure on the rifle trigger. Both men were bundled together, half on the floor between the front and back seats. One had his head twisted in the awkward position that told of a broken neck. The other one was groaning. Stark reached in through the open window and grabbed a fistful of his hair. He jerked up and twisted, raising the head and turning the face towards him.

Somebody, perhaps the man himself, had held a rifle in a bad position and angle when the car hit the rock. The man had been slammed down against the muzzle with sufficient force to impale himself on the barrel. It had burst through his cheek and ripped a great gouge in the roof of his mouth. By jerking up his head, Stark had lifted the man off the rifle. The barrel gleamed dully with the blood, thick near the muzzle and trickling down the barrel in tiny rivulets. A flap of crimson-dripping flesh hung away from the cheek. The shrill scream emitted by the injured man allowed Stark to see the wound inside his mouth. The agony glittered in his eyes, reflected in the glow from the headlights bounced off the rain-slick rock.

He wouldn't have died from the wounds. The gouge in the roof of his mouth would have healed and, with cosmetic surgery, there might not even have been a visible scar where his cheek was torn open. But Stark had a grip on him and he was a company man: so he had to die. He screamed, he coughed and he gagged. But the two wounds continued to pump out blood while Stark kept the man's head forced back. His lungs filled with the thick crimson and he drowned.

It didn't take long. But long enough for the headlights of a cluster of vehicles to show through the rain, heading north from the direction of Sault Ste. Marie. The lights might or might not have signalled the approach of company reinforcements – enforcers to give help if it was needed and undertakers to clear up the refuse of violence. Stark did not wait around to find out. He thrust the rifle he had used into the Range Rover and went to the Ford with its engine still ticking over. He kept the lights out until he had driven around the curve. The fact that he had left his suitcases in the wrecked Chevrolet occurred to him, but his only regret about the oversight was that the luggage held dry clothes. The ones he wore steamed as the Ford's heater made itself felt. The rain continued to lash down, gusted by wild wind currents whipped through the mountain crags. No headlights hung in the reflection of the rear-view mirror. He had the time and opportunity to experience the discomfort of cold flesh in clammy wet clothing, and to suffer the aches and pains of countless bruises.

But thinking about his misery did nothing to alleviate it. So he tried to ignore it by recalling the sight of the dead men littering the curve of the highway many miles behind him. It helped. Recalling Belinda Jarratt's full-bodied nakedness sprawled across the office desk and the slender firmness of Inga Ohlson spread-eagled on the double bed in the hotel room acted as an even stronger palliative.

'There's got to be something more to life than screwing and killing, mate,' he told himself, and the weariness in his voice made him realise abruptly how tired he was. He laughed. 'Something that doesn't leave you feeling shagged out.'

CHAPTER ELEVEN

CAPITAN was thirty miles north of Edmonton. At its centre it still preserved a few small cabins and a larger store converted into a miniature museum as proof that the town had been founded by the overlanders more than a century previously. Perhaps, on occasions, a tourist made a mistake and forked off the main road to Lesser Slave Lake and the Alaska Highway and actually visited the museum. But, for the most part, Capitan remained a backwater town where the retired rich came to die and the working rich returned to sleep each night, after making more dollars for a day's labour in Edmonton. Some of the latter group commuted by car. Others used the railroad which wound a tortuous route from Edmonton to Dawson Creek, across the provincial boundary in British Columbia.

Stark took the train: in the early evening of the day following the ambush under the shadow of Batchawana Mountain. He had made good time, without the need to sacrifice sleep for mileage. At first, there had been just a short rest – a couple of hours curled up on the rear seat of the Ford halted at the edge of Pukaskwa National Park, west of Wawa, on the lake front. In Thunder Bay, he had found a young charter pilot with a Cessna Golden Eagle who needed five hundred dollars before a maintenance crew at the local airport would repair his engine. Stark had an idea he was being rooked, but nonetheless paid the pilot another two hundred and fifty bucks for fuel to fly him to the big commercial airport at Edmonton. He slept most of the way.

There were two short stops. First, at Winnipeg, when the engine was giving trouble. Then at Saskatoon for refuelling. Stark got his moneysworth for the trip by asking the pilot to let him out of the aircraft on the far side of the field from the terminal complex. He made the request with the Colt

Commander resting against the man's hip. He didn't think the pilot could cause police trouble, because he had more than an idea the man used his 'plane for other than strictly legal purposes. He was willing to take a chance on news of the incident reaching company ears: considering there was less risk this way than by leaving the airport via the public exit.

He caught a local bus into the city centre, bought a map from a news-stand and decided to take the train out to the town where Dan Groves lived. Whichever route he chose had the inbuilt risk that the company was sure to have Groves under surveillance. He could only hope that would not become a problem until he was a lot closer to his objective.

He got aboard the six-thirty local and it was the same as getting a similarly timed train out of London's Waterloo Station. It was tight packed with weary-eyed men, some of them breathing out liquor fumes, and brighter looking women, freshly made-up and perfumed after the typewriters and adding machines had been covered.

It was a stop-start journey, with passengers getting off at the suburban stations and hardly anybody else getting on. Nobody gave Stark more than a second glance, which was a tribute to Groves' taste in clothes and ability to pay highly for them. For despite the soaking Stark had taken the previous night, the suit had dried without wrinkling and the mud stains had brushed off.

Once the coal and oil town of Edmonton was left behind, the train started to make better time through the agricultural belt. Stark felt less at ease when the open-plan car became sparsely populated. But having a hand inside his jacket, fisted around the cold steel of the Colt Commander stuck in his waistband, enabled him to keep the wariness out of his expression.

The Capitan depot was on the town's central square which was formed by the timber buildings preserved from the nineteenth century and the very twentieth-century business premises: a supermarket, a bank, a service station and a post office. When the train pulled into the depot to disembark most of its remaining passengers, the afternoon was giving its final gasp of light and evening was full-born. Street lamps were on around the square and a few neon signs were discreetly lit without flashing. Stark stepped down from the train in the centre of a group of tired-looking businessmen and raked his eyes over a thousand shadowed places. He paid no heed to his imagination. Just stayed tense and poised to move fast if danger threatened.

Three cabs were quickly claimed. Other men slid into waiting cars and were driven home by their wives. Still more dispersed across the parking lot and drove themselves. The train had already pulled out and Stark decided against trying for a car. While his fellow passengers were getting into their own vehicles there was a risk one of them would spot him as an intruder stealing a friend's car. Capitan was that small a town. And, after they had gone, the parking lot became a dangerous wasteland of exposed tarmac scattered spartanly with crouching cars. He would be too long in the open reaching any one of them.

He went into a telephone booth and checked the local directory. The listing as *Mr. and Mrs. Daniel P. Groves* was intriguing. The address of the Groves' residence was one-eighty-seven Oak Tree Road. The man in the depot ticket window eyed him curiously as he stepped out of the booth. He was an old man wearing spectacles with thick lenses which magnified the look in his eyes.

'Can I help you, sir?' he asked in a tone which said he was very anxious to be of assistance.

One of the cabs returned to park in its marked slot immediately outside the broad entrance of the depot. Then a second taxi. Or Stark thought it was until he did a double take. It wasn't a sign on the roof. It was an unilluminated light. And the crest on the opening door marked it as a patrol unit of the Canadian Mounted Police.

Stark had two alternatives. To lunge into a run and certainly arouse suspicion. Or to play it cool. He elected the second course because it gave him the option of taking the first if the breaks went the wrong way.

He ambled across to the ticket window, and showed the old man an anxious smile. 'I was supposed to be met here.'

'You English?' His smile was bright and interested.

Stark nodded and glanced casually over his shoulder. The cop, who wore sergeant's stripes, was talking with the cab driver. They found something to laugh about.

'Got an English family living on Rockland Avenue. Run the Downtown Restaurant. Been here ten years. Name of James. Laurence and Elizabeth. Come from Hertfordshire. They who you come to town to see?'

'No. Daniel P. Groves.'

The old man nodded, light flashing on his spectacle lenses. A draught streamed into the depot as one of the plate glass doors was opened.

'Lives out on Oak Tree Road at the north end of town.'

'I just telephoned the house. There's no reply. I was supposed to have been met.'

'Evening, Ray.'

'Mr. Dwyer.' The Mountie wore the traditional red uniform jacket. But the dark trousers and peaked cap marred the image. His forty-year-old face was all cop. It bore the international stamp of hard, miss-nothing eyes and a mouthline that looked tough even when he was smiling. He smiled at Stark as he nodded to him.

'Guy from England, Ray. Waiting to be met from Mr. Groves' house.'

The copper's eyes surveyed Stark again and he thrust a hand into his jacket pocket, making sure the outline of the revolver did not show. The Colt Commander at his hip was screened by the loose drape of the jacket.

'Cab'll get you there in ten minutes, young feller,' Dwyer said.

'Thought the Oak Tree Road house was closed up,' the Mountie put in, his second survey producing a negative print-out in his copper's mind behind the hard eyes. 'Last I heard Mr. Groves was in Europe.'

'He came back,' Stark said.

'Maybe he didn't arrive yet. Explain why there's nobody to meet you and the 'phone didn't answer.'

Stark felt a little light-headed, as if he wasn't in a real situation at all. Rather, that this was a sequence from a particularly vivid dream. The depot lights seemed too bright. The plate glass doors were too highly polished. The old man at the ticket window and the loose-limbed Mountie were making too much of the whole thing. There were too many shadowed places out on the square. The shadows growing darker as the evening advanced and the street lamps and neon signs glowed more harshly.

'Tell you what I'll do,' the Mountie said. 'I'm scheduled to take a run through the north side. Part of my route is along Oak Tree Road. I'll ride you up there. Mr. Dwyer, if somebody comes to meet Mr. . . . ?'

The English couple living in Capitan came from Hertfordshire. In the days when Stark had friends, one of them had lived in Hertfordshire. In a village called Stanstead Abbotts. 'Stanley Abbott,' he supplied.

'Mr. Abbott, you tell them I've taken him out to the house,' the Mountie finished.

The dreamlike quality was heightened. Even his voice had an odd sound to his own ears as he replied: 'Thanks a lot.'

'Certainly do that, Ray,' the old man called as the Mountie headed for the door and Stark found himself following automatically.

But, as he moved around the patrol car and sank into the front passenger seat, the logic of what was happening imprinted reality over the odd sense of detachment. Capitan was a small town where few trains stopped. A quiet residential town with a low crime rate. The railroad man and the Mountie were under-employed. A stranger where few were ever seen was a time-filling curiosity.

'Know Canada at all, Mr. Abbott?' the Mountie asked

after he had reversed the car away from the cab stand in front of the depot and was steering it around the square.

'First time here,' Stark told him. 'Only arrived a couple of days ago.'

The lights were going out in the supermarket. Somewhere a clock struck the quarter. The police car swung off the square and started along a street which ran north. The driver asked a stream of questions about Stark's first impressions of the country. Then he changed the subject to England. He knew a detective on the Birmingham city police force. Fortunately, Stark had been to Birmingham a few times. He was able to respond to the questions in the same manner they were asked – with easy friendliness which left no uneasy pauses.

At the same time he could pretend a casual interest in the street scenes while actually maintaining a careful surveillance on the changing surroundings. The downtown area was small. Main Street, along which they were travelling, quickly ran out of shops, offices, restaurants and bars. Then it became Maple Avenue, tree-lined and flanked by expensive-looking houses. As the car continued its arrow-straight, northbound journey, the houses became larger, more widely spaced and more heavily screened. Traffic was light as the dinner hour approached. No car followed the police unit as it made a left turn off Maple Avenue on to a sweeping crescent with a lamp standard sign naming it as Oak Tree Road.

'Business acquaintance of Mr. Groves?' the Mountie asked, suddenly switching the easy conversation away from Birmingham City Football Club.

'I'm going to see him about a few loose ends on a contract,' Stark replied truthfully.

'He's a nice guy to do business with, I reckon. Nice guy all round. I guess you know he's big on charity?'

'I've heard.'

'It's a stinking, lousy, rotten world.' He slowed the car as they reached the top of a gentle rise. 'Mr. Groves being such a nice guy and then for that to happen to his wife.'

Stark didn't know what the copper was talking about. 'That's the way it goes,' he responded balefully.

'Here it is – and he is at home, looks like.'

It was a large, brick-built house in the British Victorian style. It stood fifty yards back from the road behind a square of lawn featured with neatly edged flower beds and a central fountain stained with old water marks. A hedge guarded the house from the prying eyes of passers-by on the street. It grew to a height of ten feet. There was just a single entrance which could be closed off by a wrought iron gate. The gate was now open and as the police car rolled through, on to a tarmac driveway that skirted the lawn, Stark and the driver could see lights on in the house. It was subdued by the curtains hung at two windows on the lower floor. But a bright wedge fell through the open front door, down three steps and across the broad apron of tarmac fronting the porch.

A panel truck was parked there, with the rear doors opened. The legend on the side of the truck proclaimed EDMONTON EXPRESS DELIVERY SERVICE. Two men were lifting a large wooden crate from the rear of the truck. They wore white coveralls with identical lettering emblazoned across their backs. Dan Groves, dressed in pyjamas, carpet slippers and a robe stood on the threshold of the house. He was pale faced and his pallor grew worse when he saw the police car roll to a halt in the patch of light. The delivery men continued with their chore after casting indifferent glances towards the official vehicle.

'Evening, Mr. Groves,' the Mountie called cheerfully through his wound-down window. 'Brought you a visitor.'

The cop stayed at the wheel.

'Thanks for the lift, mate,' Stark told him, and got out quickly. 'It's Stan Abbott, Mr. Groves,' he called before the man in the doorway had a chance to use the wrong name in greeting him. 'I telephoned from the station.'

A man doesn't get to be the head of a nationwide industrial complex unless he is bright. Groves showed his quick thinking ability and combined it with a seemingly effortless change of expression – spreading a welcoming smile over his pale face.

'I was in the shower and the bathroom extension's on the blink. Come on in, Stan. Appreciate your giving my guest a ride, Ray.'

'Pleasure, sir.' The Mountie waved to take in Groves and Stark, then gunned his engine and swerved around the panel truck to leave the front of the house by way of the far side of the lawn.

Groves continued his faked mood for the benefit of the deliverymen, shaking Stark's hand and opening a light line of small talk. Then he gave instructions for the crate – some six feet long by three feet wide and deep – to be carried to the kitchen. He shot an anxious glance at Stark, then followed the white-clad men along the oak-panelled hallway and through a double doorway beneath a balcony formed where the two wings of the flying staircase met.

Stark closed the door before bringing up the rear. The kitchen was an enormous room, tight-packed around all the walls with units and equipment. Virgin white and blood red. After the crate had been set down on the tiled floor alongside an eating bar, Groves had to go in search of his trousers for money to pay the deliverymen for their trouble. He took less than a minute. Stark spent the time eyeing the crate, which looked innocent enough, unless one had reason to be concerned with death. He could not help thinking that the crate had the dimensions and shape of a crude coffin.

'Are you crazy?' Groves demanded angrily.

The sound of the panal truck's engine diminished into the chill night. Stark was just lighting a cigarette. 'Maybe,' he said on a cloud of smoke.

'They must be watching the house, now they know I'm in contact with you.'

Stark nodded. 'Right, mate. And I had the crazy luck of a police escort right up to the front door. Crazy luck for a man who's crazy.'

'What do you want?'

'To get out of Canada after I've finished the job. Like they say in the spy books, my cover's blown. Ever since I got away from the riding lodge place, I've stayed only one step ahead of the company. After I've done what you want doing, I want my escape route open and all systems at go.'

'Why didn't you telephone? It would have been safer.' Despite his fearful dismay at Stark's presence, Groves was more than a little preoccupied with the newly delivered crate. His frightened gaze kept straying to it.

'Some telephone lines are like some walls, Mr. Groves,' Stark said. 'They have ears. Why don't you open it up?'

He tapped the crate with a toe of his shoe. It was packed tightly. No hollow ring. The way the men had carried it had shown it was heavy.

'I've got a bad feeling about it,' Groves said. He looked a lot older now. Ten years more than when Stark had last seen him on the roof of the Faversham Hotel. And that had been a bad time.

Stark nodded. 'At the fee you're paying, I can afford to give you the occasional free service.'

He opened a lot of unit drawers before finding the one in which the cutlery was stored. He took out a sturdy carving knife and a length of whetstone. The carving knife blade prised up the lid of the crate a fraction of an inch before it snapped. But then there was enough of a gap to insert the whetstone and lift it some more. The nails creaked as they were withdrawn from the wood. Stark used his fingers hooked under the boards to open the lid the whole way.

Groves staggered backwards and hit his hip against the edge of the eating bar. His gaunt face was so pale now that even his lips looked white beneath the harsh fluorescent strip lighting of the big kitchen.

'Bill!' he gasped, and a shudder vibrated his entire body.

The youngster was naked and there was not a mark on his body or head to show how he had died. And no way to tell how long he had been dead. He looked as if he might have been pumped full of embalming fluid. Or maybe it was just the preserving effect of the ice that had held back decomposition. The ice was all around him. Some of it had melted, but not much. And there was no way the water could run away for the ice and the corpse were encased in a clear polythene bag with the opening sealed up.

Stark looked down impassively upon the latest intrusion of death into his life and then he sighed. 'Looks like you've been to a lot of trouble and expense for nothing, mate,' he said softly, glancing up at Groves. The older man met his gaze with eyes which demanded the answer to a tacit, horrified question. Stark shook his head. 'No, it wasn't me. I do my job without fancy trimmings.'

The thought that Stark had been responsible for the gruesome delivery had caused anger to feed strength into Groves' body. Now he sagged against the bar again. Then managed to hoist himself on to a high backed stool to keep from collapsing entirely.

'But he was killed because I brought you to Canada,' Groves groaned.

'I'm making no charge for that,' Stark told him, and was about to allow the lid to fall back into place when he saw an envelope Scotchtaped to the underside. When he tore it free, a folded sheet of paper fluttered to the polythene shroud encasing the corpse. The envelope hung by a corner and he could read the name GROVES printed on it. He picked up the paper, and made to hand it towards Groves as he covered the crude coffin with its lid. 'Maybe the delivery note explains it.'

Groves had withdrawn into the privacy of his own thoughts. He came out of it with a start, and shook his head when he saw the paper. 'You read it. I can't.'

He probably meant he was in no mental condition to assimilate the written word. The sheened glaze of ready-to-spill tears sheeting his grey eyes probably meant he wasn't seeing too clearly, anyway. The paper was quarto size, folded twice. The message was short, printed in block capitals with a felt-tipped pen:

YOU BROUGHT US A PACKAGE WE DIDN'T WANT. WE RECIPROCATE.

Stark scanned the words, then read them aloud to Groves. 'Seems they boobed,' he said. 'You've got exactly what you want.'

The tears spilled from the glazed eyes and Groves folded forward across the eating bar, resting his forehead on his folded arms. The sobs shook his body. Stark crossed to the double sink unit, ran water on the tip of his cigarette and pushed the messy result into the waste-disposal. The big window behind the sinks was filled by a closed venetian blind. He wondered how many company men were out there on the other side of the shaded window. Not in the whole of Canada. Just here, in Capitan, in the vicinity of the house.

Not many, yet. A house on a residential street was not a good surveillance subject. You couldn't watch it with too many men without arousing suspicion. And, as he had surmised earlier, the company would not expect him to come here. But they wouldn't leave it entirely uncovered. The word would now be out that Stark had again made contact with Groves. The executives would be surprised, but not paralysed. Reinforcements would even now be moving towards Capitan. Which meant Stark had no more time to waste listening to Groves bawling about something he had wanted to happen anyway.

But, as he spun away from the sinks, Groves stopped of his own accord. He was sitting upright on the stool, staring at the wallpaper which showed a design of herbs.

'My wife hanged herself,' he said softly. 'Six months ago. Two weeks after I had her committed to a mental institution in Montreal.'

'We all have our problems,' Stark replied coldly. 'Right now I need to know about my escape route.'

'Listen!' Groves snapped, then adjusted his voice to the same monotone level as before. 'My wife – Bill's mother – went out of her mind when she discovered she'd been married to a man for thirty years who had been unfaithful to her from the start. And not just plain, straightforward unfaithful to her. You saw what kind of a girl Belinda Jarratt was. They were all like that. When a man is rich, he can afford to indulge his whims.'

'Money bought Belinda – loyalty and all?'

'Could there be anything else with a man like me? She was special, but only because I paid her the best.'

'That was why junior here went on his kinky sex binge?'

'He loved his mother. Nothing abnormal. They were just very close. Quite rightly, he blamed me for her death. He accused me of being depraved. And he said that because he had my blood in his veins, he could be just as depraved. I'm a solid citizen, Mr. Stark. A pillar of respectability. He knew that even if he'd gone on a coast-to-coast television show to denounce me, nobody would have believed a word he said. So he tried to ruin me by covering himself in the same kind of dirt I've been grovelling in for so long.'

'I thought sex scandals only hurt politicians and clergymen,' Stark said lightly. It was an effort to moderate his tone. Time was running out, but he was forced to acknowledge that Groves had the whiphand. With the boy already quite literally on ice, Stark had nothing with which to bargain. Except maybe Groves' life: but he had more than an idea that the man wasn't too concerned with self-preservation at the moment.

'My private life is just one part of me, Mr. Stark,' Groves said, turning to slide off the stool. He grimaced. 'A man does not live by perverted screwing alone. Some men might be satisfied with that plus the satisfaction of controlling a massive industrial chain. But I also need the kudos of my reputation. I enjoy being respected to the same extent as I derive pleasure from women like Belinda Jarratt. I think I need it even more.'

He was moving about the kitchen, walking around it and across it; always taking care to avoid the crate containing the body of his son. 'So much so that, when I received some photographs showing my boy with grotesque harridans –

making perverted love to them – I allowed the company to move in on Groves Industries.'

Stark was getting the story he had come to hear. Only one issue needed clarification now. Groves filled the gap without prompting.

'And then I suddenly realised what I was doing. If those photographs ever became public property, just one part of my life would suffer. But to become known for links with the company – that could ruin me completely and utterly. Prison, perhaps. That is why I decided to have Bill eliminated. Mud seldoms sticks to the newly dead.'

He stopped his aimless wanderings, looked at the floor and sighed. Then he raised his gaze to find Stark. The grey eyes were clear once more.

'One of the reasons I came here was to ask the questions you've just answered,' Stark told him. 'I'm not going to pretend that I understand a man like you. But it doesn't matter.'

'I don't suppose it does, to you,' Groves answered. 'Except that I hope you now realise that any company connections I have were forced upon me – and that you can trust me.'

Stark shook his head as he pushed himself away from the sink unit. 'I don't have any need to trust you, mate. Because you don't owe me anything. You got me out of Sweden when it was about time I made a move. Smashing the company wherever and whenever I can is what I do anyway. So whatever trouble I've had doesn't involve you in debt. You brought me over to do a job and now I'm redundant. I'm not going to twist your arm to get a golden handshake.'

Groves pointed at the crate. His face was set in a hard expression, but his hand shook a little. 'I loved that boy. Despite everything else. I loved him. I loved his mother, too. And I killed them both. As surely as if I had tied them to a wall and shot them to pieces with a machine gun. And I've got to live with that knowledge. For a while.'

The final two words were soft spoken: almost inaudible.

'I'd be glad if you say what you have to say quickly,' Stark urged.

Groves lowered his pointing hand and gave a terse nod. 'Of course. They'll be on the way, won't they. For you, and maybe for me, too. Will you come with me?'

He didn't wait for a reply. He swung around and strode purposefully out of the kitchen and along the elegant hallway. With Stark close behind him, he swung through an archway into a narrow passage at one side. The door at the end was locked.

'I've left the key upstairs,' he said, and stood back. 'Would you, please?'

Stark shrugged, bent a knee and crashed the heel of his shoe against the lock. It was an internal door and its security was not good. It crashed open. Groves nodded his thanks and stepped through. He pulled a cord and two long fluorescent tubes flickered and steadied. They illuminated a four car garage which smelled of fresh oil and old exhaust fumes. A Lincoln Continental and a Jensen Interceptor occupied two stalls. A third was empty. The fourth, across the vacant space, was taken up by a battered and rust-speckled Plymouth Barracuda that looked at least five ill-used years old.

As Groves led the way around the front of the gleaming limousines, a thought occurred to him. 'I don't suppose you've had the time to listen to the radio or read newspapers?'

'There must be more peaceful ways to travel through Canada,' Stark allowed wryly.

'The chauffeur – the man who was supposed to meet you at Toronto airport. The police found his body on the railroad tracks outside Oshawa. They think it was an accident. That he fell in front of an express.'

'You knew all about me when you found me, Mr. Groves,' Stark said. 'You knew the risks.'

The older man nodded as he took a key ring from a hook on a shelf. 'The chauffeur's death is just one other reason why I wish you to continue working for me. Bill, first. Then my wife. Belinda and that poor man whose name I do not even know.'

He fitted a key into the boot lock of the Barracuda and sprang open the lid.

'Christ!' Stark said.

'I did not just sit and wait for you to contact me, Mr. Stark,' Groves said evenly.

The boot of the car held a miniature arsenal. Two automatic rifles – an A-R 18 calibre 5·56 mm and a 7·62 mm G-3. A Luger Naval Parabellum, a Walther P.38 and two ·357 Combat Magnums took care of the handgun department. A box of US issue grenades and two cartons of explosives. A Schmeisser MP40 submachine gun and a Savage 7 mm sporting rifle fitted with a telescopic sight. And, of course, ample shells for all the guns.

'Don't be fooled by the bodyshell of the car, Mr. Stark,' Groves said, and his voice had become a little dull – disinterested. 'It comes off a three year old Plymouth. But it is built on to a truck chassis. The engine comes from a late model Jaguar E-Type and all necessary modifications have been made to the transmission and suspension to make allowances for the power unit.'

Stark opened the driver's door to examine the dashboard layout. It looked standard to a production line Barracuda, although he didn't know what that looked like anyway.

'The licence plates were, of course, honestly come by,' Groves said. 'But I cannot guarantee the police will be unsuspicious of the engine and chassis number. In the glove compartment there is ten thousand dollars in used bills. Half Canadian and half US. A British and a Canadian passport lacking only the same kind of information as that given to you in Stockholm. A British and an International Driver's Licence which need filling out – and a photograph for the latter, of course.'

He seemed to become more bored with each word he spoke, and breathed a gentle sigh of relief when he had said his piece.

'Just two questions,' Stark said.

'Yes?'

'Who's the target now?'

'Whoever you choose, son,' Groves said wearily, massaging his temple as if he had a nagging ache. 'Anyone you creamed between Toronto and here was just in passing. I'd like you to really lay into them now. With the weapons I've given you, so that when I read about it and see it on tee vee, I'll . . .' His voice trailed away and his clear eyes showed sadness. 'Just so I can feel I'm partially responsible for what's happening to them. And the other question?'

Stark waved a hand to encompass the car and its lethal cargo. Then he shrugged. 'Forget it, mate,' he said, slammed the boot and took the keys from the lock. 'It's here. How you got it doesn't matter. How you were going to get it to Baffin Island if I happened to call from there doesn't matter.'

'One word answer,' Groves said as Stark slid behind the wheel, closed the door and rolled down the window. 'Money.'

Stark nodded, and halted his hand as he fitted the key into the ignition. 'Anything for me in the Edmonton Express Delivery Service?' he asked.

'It's a reputable company known throughout southern Alberta.'

Stark nodded. 'Just a longshot. I guess they wouldn't use one of their own front operations to make that kind of a delivery.'

'I'm sorry I can give you no further help, son,' Groves said, meaning it.

'There's one other thing you can do,' Stark told him.

'Yes?'

'Open the door and let the Barracuda see the bait.'

CHAPTER TWELVE

THE more than four litres of power under the flaked and rusting bonnet made a raucous burst of sound as it came to life within the confines of the garage. Then it settled down to a throaty throbbing cadence and Stark curled back his lips in a grin of anticipation. When he hit the light switch as Groves rolled open the up-and-over door, he discovered something the Canadian had not told him about. The hybrid car had been fitted with more powerful headlights than would have been standard for the shell.

Stark checked the easy movement of the gear change, then eased the car forward out of the garage. He caught a brief glimpse of Groves. The man stood, partially slumped, with a hand raised weakly in farewell. It may have been a forced smile or a grimace of anguish that held his mouth in a ricture. Stark did not take a long enough or a close enough look at him. When he had driven out of the garage, he glanced at the rear-view mirror and saw the door swinging down to close.

If he had cared, Stark may have wondered about the depths of Groves' sadness and may have attached significance to something the man had said: *I've got to live with that knowledge – for a while.* Recalled, as ominous, the way in which Groves' voice had trailed away as he spoke of reading and seeing the news of what Stark was going to do to the company. But Stark didn't care. Groves had served his purpose and Stark had everything he wanted: a fast car, a lead to the company and the weaponry to hit the enemy hard. All this, and something else: the most important factor for his peace of mind. He was on his own again and accountable to no one.

Thus, as he drove slowly along the tarmac surface skirting the square of lawn to get the feel for handling the car, Stark thought only of himself. Behind him, in the closed garage, Dan Groves knew he could trust the young Englishman. He knew Stark's acts of revenge were totally selfish, but when the enemy was a common one the motivation of the weapon did not matter. So long as it killed, the object was achieved.

Groves closed the door with the broken lock, then started the engines of the Jensen and the Lincoln. He switched off the strip lights and sat down with his back against the rear wall of the garage. Newly created carbon monoxide fumed from the exhaust pipes of the two cars just a few feet from where Groves sat. He breathed the poisonous air deep into his lungs and thought about all the women in his life ... there were a lot of women and not much life left.

The two company enforcers were sitting in a souped-up Mini parked at the mouth of a narrow lane that cut off Oak Tree Road, a hundred and fifty yards east of Groves' house. They were joined by a third before Stark had reached the road from the house. This man had been crouched in the shrubbery of a garden immediately across from where the driveway reached the gated opening in the tall hedge. He had seen the garage door opened by Groves and knew the driver of the beat-up Plymouth could be nobody else but Stark. There was no time to get word to the man watching the rear of the house. As the Plymouth swept past, heading down the curving sweep of Oak Tree towards Maple, the Mini turned out of the lane. The driver kept his hands on the wheel. His two passengers – one seated beside him and the second in the rear seat – drew Colt ·45 automatics from hip holsters.

Stark was aware of the car behind him but made no attempt to lose the tail in town. He turned south on to Maple and the street became busy, by Capitan standards, as it ran through the downtown area of Main. Cars were parked nose-in to the kerb outside the bars and restaurants and there were strollers on the sidewalks. There was a queue of people moving slowly into the theatre on the square. Cars moved slowly as their drivers searched for parking spaces. Others headed out of town. The Mountie who rode a patrol car instead of a horse was talking to the group of cab drivers outside the railroad depot.

Going around the square, the Mini's headlights flashed. One of the cab drivers detached himself from the group and went into the depot. Stark caught a glimpse of the man easing into the telephone booth. He guessed that within minutes a hold order would be sent out to the enforcers heading for Capitan.

The highway stretching south towards Edmonton ran parallel with the railroad he had travelled earlier that day. Clear of the town's speed restriction he took advantage of the freedom: but not to lose the tail. Merely to test the car's handling at high speed and to make sure there was just the single vehicle covering him. Of the light traffic making for the city, only the Mini stayed with him. His own car swayed and vibrated a little on the sharper curves, but the wide tread tyres remained firmly in contact with the paving. And he got instant reponse from the engine, steering and transmission as his sensitive hands made expert use of the controls. He didn't test the brakes until later.

The high speed – varying between eighty and a hundred – quickly took Stark and his tail far ahead of the Edmonton-bound traffic. So far, no vehicles had swept past in the opposite direction.

The side road which veered off to the east could be seen from a mile back down the highway. A three-quarter moon shining down from a cloudless sky spread a soft, silver-blue light across the flat prairie land. It showed a line of telegraph poles and glinted on the wires strung between. A reflective directional sign at the shoulder of the main highway announced that the road to Redwater cut off to the left. So far, Stark had done nothing to alert the enforcers to his awareness of their proximity. He didn't now.

Easing back his speed gradually, he used the left side blinkers to signal his intention, and swung sedately into the turn. The Mini closed up the distance on the Plymouth as the two cars gained speed along the side road. Stark, his steady gaze flickering between the rear-view mirror and the road, waited for the Mini to nudge up to within a hundred feet of his rear bumper. Then, with a grunt of pleasure at the response, he dropped down a gear and stomped the accelerator pedal to the floor. The roar of power was like a symphony in his ears. The adrenalin surged through him. His back sank into the seat cushioning and he took a firmer grip on the smoothness of the steering wheel.

Within seconds, the distance between the two cars had doubled. Stark thrust the gears into top and stepped on the pedal again. Behind him, the driver of the Mini and his car were slower to react. The gap continued to grow as the arrow straightness of the smooth-surfaced road allowed Stark to push his speed to the one hundred and fifty miles an hour maximum. The engine hummed as sweetly as when it was giving sixty.

But Stark did not overplay his hand. He held the top speed for only a few minutes. Then he eased back on the pedal, allowing the dots of the following headlights to grow larger in the smoked glass of the rear-view mirror. But not too large. He adjusted his speed until he discovered the Mini's maximum was about a hundred and ten and was able to stay a constant half mile ahead of the following car.

They were travelling through the farm belt with acres of wheat fields stretching away on either side of the road: the new crop sprouting green, and sparkling with the sheen of evening dew. But nature does not remain regimented even on the plains of North America, and five miles from the main highway the road began to rise and dip, twist and turn through an area of rolling pasture land. Stark had passed one cluster of farm buildings dominated by two huge grain elevators. Then, cresting a rise, he saw the lights of another farm, far ahead. He decided to make his move before he reached them.

The opportunity was presented at the foot of the downgrade and now he tested the brakes. He hit the pedal hard at a hundred miles an hour going into a bend. Burning rubber screamed and the car tried to go into a spin. He pumped into cadence braking, easing the wheel around to keep the front end of the car angling into the bend. Then, as the road straightened, he released the foot brake and jerked on the parking brake. His left hand wrenched over the wheel.

More black rubber was seared into the paving as the car lurched into a controlled side-slide. The car did a complete about-face and came to a halt on the right side of the road. Its headlights blazed at the bend for a moment before Stark hit the switch. He snatched the keys from the ignition and flung open the door. The only sound from the car was the angry tick of cooling metal. He smelt hot rubber as he keyed open the boot. And, lifting out the Schmeisser, he smelt himself. The sweat of excited anticipation. It oozed from every pore in his body and adhered to his underwear and to his flesh. For the first time since Groves had put up the proposition, Stark was going to hit the company at a time and a place he had chosen. All the previous skirmishes had been defensive, his tactics and actions dictated by factors beyond his control.

The moment of exhilaration over, Stark became as cold as the metal of the submachine gun in his hands. The sweat seemed to turn to ice: his mind worked with the same brand of well-oiled smoothness as the gun's action as he slotted in the thirty-two round magazine and cocked the weapon. He crouched down beside the front nearside wing of the car, leaning against the rust-pitted metal of the bodyshell. Already he could see the headlight beams of the Mini probing into the clear night sky as the tiny car raced up to the crest of the low hill.

It came over the hump with all four wheels clear of the road. But it landed on a straight course to barrel down the hill. The range was too long, but Stark kept the Schmeisser trained on the speeding car, the pistol grip nestling comfortably in his palm as his index finger took first pressure around the trigger. Because of the curve at the foot of the slope there was no danger of being dazzled while the Mini took the downgrade. The car was almost on level ground, on the point of veering to take the bend, when its brake lights splashed a vivid glow behind it and the engine whined. The degree of curve didn't merit such harsh braking and Stark knew the crouching shape of the Plymouth had been spotted.

He squeezed the trigger.

The range was fifty yards and the target was moving. But the range was closing and the target was large. He didn't even try for specific hits as the gun trembled with rapid fire. He merely eased the barrel back and forth across a short arc, swinging his body slightly to stay sideways on to the car. A tyre burst, the lights went out and the driver died. The engine stopped and hot oil sprayed. The Mini was held on the road for a moment longer, as the enforcer in the front passenger seat grabbed the wheel. But then a shard of flying glass sank deep into an eye and he covered his face with both hands. The man in the rear seat threw himself across the upholstery and curled into a ball. The final arc of the machine gun sent a stream of bullets through the bodywork of the out-of-control Mini. They had enough velocity to smash through his hands and arms and shattered his skull. The car, powered by it own momentum, crashed into the low banking on the outside of the bend. The front end reared up, bumper and radiator grille hanging off. The ticking of its cooling engine was the only sound in the countryside for stretched seconds as the car balanced on its rear end. Then it toppled backwards across the road, its roof collapsing with the agonised tearing sound of telescoping metal and the counterpoint of tinkling glass. It became still.

Stark straightened up from his crouching posture and a bone in his leg creaked as the tension drained out of him. His face felt stiff and he had to make a physical effort to alter the lines of the killer's grin that had masked his features while his finger was pressuring the trigger. The anti-climax of violence was short-lived and he slid into smooth, loose-limbed action again; going to the rear of the car, locking the big gun back into the boot and then getting behind the wheel. The engine fired first time. The wrecked Mini, crushed, pitted with bullet holes and leaking its life blood of oil and petrol, partially blocked the road. Stark nudged the Plymouth into the crippled car, spinning it gently out of his path. Bone crunched and flesh squelched as moving metal ground into the dead bodies.

Stark glanced out at the oil and mud-caked exposed underbelly of the upside-down car and now his grin was of quiet pleasure. 'Never was sold on the Minis,' he muttered. 'Always were inclined to get twitchy when you gave them the gun.'

He roared the Plymouth back along the road through the pasture land and wheat fields towards the main highway into Edmonton.

Far to the north west, high in the Sharktooth Mountains close to British Columbia's border with the Yukon, Rick Essex endeavoured to put the Revenger out of his mind as he showed Angelo Spagnoli over Snowy Ridge.

'Every woman, no matter what her age or appearance, is constantly prepared to be persuaded she is beautiful.'

The speaker was a very beautiful woman herself, who moved and spoke in a way which suggested she was fully confident of her own attractiveness. She spoke from a raised dais at one end of a long room furnished as a lecture hall. On the dais was a small table for two set with silver cutlery and bone china, lit by candles and decorated with a vase of flowers. The woman, who was about thirty, swayed sensuously back and forth across the dais behind the table. The class she was addressing comprised ten young men who occupied the front tier of chairs. Essex and Spagnoli stood at the back of the room, just inside the door.

'You can help her to convince herself both by words and actions,' the unlikely looking tutor continued. 'When you are alone with her in the privacy of a bedroom, words spoken with a sincere tone may suffice. But in public places, a glimpse of herself under bad lighting in a carelessly placed mirror can ruin the lie. Always endeavour to take your escort to a discreetly lit restaurant or bar. Candlelight is preferable to electric light. Never go into places illuminated by fluorescent . . .'

'And that woman's a whore in one of your Vancouver houses?' Spagnoli asked, amazed, as he spun out through the doorway.

Essex nodded as he closed the door to block off the lecturer's voice. He smiled with pride. 'That's right, Angelo. All the girls we use at Snowy Ridge are from the company's vice circuit.' He laughed. 'From the top end, of course. The boys deserve to train with the best before they go out into the field and have to ball the ugly old biddies. And we also use this place as a rest and recreation centre for the fully trained fellers. The way we figure it, the guys would go nuts if they didn't get in some sack time with younger nooky from time to time. So, every three months, they get the chance to come up here if they want.'

'That's a nice idea,' Spagnoli congratulated. 'I like that, Rick. I like the whole operation.'

The US syndicate man was a third generation American. His accent was West Coast university, and an heritance of non-Latin blood from a white Russian grandmother had contributed strongly to the moulding of his features. His eyes were dark and his nose had something of the Roman cast to it, but otherwise there was nothing particularly Italian about him except his name. He was just the wrong side of fifty and still carried his six feet, well-built frame in an upright posture. He wore a hairpiece, but it was a high-price one, exactly matching the mixture of grey and black of the natural growth in which it was set.

His energy seemed as boundless as his enthusiasm for the Canadian company's male prostitution operation. And Rick Essex was grateful to his visitor for this. Charlie Swenson had not yet arrived at Snowy Ridge and Essex badly needed a substitute for the youngster's hard and inventive body in order to keep his mind preoccupied and away from Stark. He had flown his guest up from Reindeer Mountain to the airfield outside Fort Nelson. Then a helicopter had taken them on the final hop to Snowy Ridge, the most exclusive of the nationwide chain of recreational operations run by Essex Leisure Limited. Shortly after touching down on the pad which had been cleared of snow – and while the American was taking a leak – Essex had been told of the incident on the road north of Sault Ste. Marie. And for the first time, the top man of the company's Canadian arm began to worry seriously about the Revenger's presence in his territory.

Stark's score against the company was mounting and each time he hit, he vanished again without trace. Past experience – fortunately gleaned at second hand – showed the bastard did not confine himself to taking out company muscle. His ultimate targets were always the company's operations and the executives who ran them. He – Essex – was the top executive, presently at the headquarters of the male prostitution circuit which was the most lucrative spoke in the Canadian arm's wheel of crime. And Stark was heading in the general direction of Snowy Ridge.

Walking alongside Spagnoli, Essex told himself not to be a fool. So Stark was moving westwards across Canada? Canada was a big country. Snowy Ridge was in a remote corner. Stark was on the move simply because the company operation to capture him forced him on the run. The fact that he was heading west meant nothing. And yet . . . Essex still wished Charlie would hurry up and reach the mountains. He needed the boy's body and he needed the sense of security Charlie's presence gave him. A quality that would be even stronger now Charlie had proved his ability by taking out Harry Gorman.

'And the boys are taught on every aspect of behaviour here?' the American said.

The two men were strolling along a broad, well-lit corridor

running down the centre of a long, single-storey building. Doors of one piece wood and bearing only a number, lined both walls. Outside, the night temperature was ten degrees below zero and the clouds swirling around the mountain peaks threatened more snow. But inside, electric heating maintained the air at a constant seventy degrees.

'That's right,' Essex answered. 'How to talk to women, how to eat with them, travel with them, walk with them and, most important of all, how to make love to them. As you saw from the books at the Edmonton office, the special clients of Trans-Canadian pay high for the service they receive. We have to match the quantity of their money with the quality of our products.'

'You actually have classes on love-making?' Spagnoli asked, his amazement heightening.

'I thought that part of the Snowy Ridge course would interest you the most, Angelo,' Essex answered, and winked. 'That's why we've been passing all these doors. Here we are.'

He stopped before a door as anonymously numbered as all the others leading off the broad passageway. He didn't knock before opening it and ushering the American through. Essex had given the word, shortly after leaving the chopper, that there was to be no formality during the tour. Spagnoli wanted to see Snowy Ridge under normal conditions and so it had been. First in the purely recreational areas of the complex – on the ski slopes, the skating rink, the sled run, the restaurant and the bar. Then in the administration building with the offices at one end and the classrooms which took up the remainder of the accommodation.

'Wow!' the American breathed in awe as he saw what was happening through the doorway.

The teachers and pupils engaged in imparting and assimilating knowledge in this room were probably the most appreciative of the building's central heating. For most were either naked or only partially dressed. The room was four times as large as the one in which the Vancouver whore was explaining the basic principles of restaurant etiquette. And in here, the training was advanced beyond the basics. At its centre was a carousel-like construction with a desk and a control panel on one side and a curved row of seats, facing outwards, on the other. A woman sat at the desk, with one hand resting on the adjacent control panel. A dozen men – as young, well-built and good-looking as all the others Spagnoli had seen both at Reindeer Mountain and Snowy Ridge – occupied the seats. Partitions sub-divided the room on all four sides into a series of much smaller rooms, each of them open-ended – like film sets. Each of these small rooms was fully furnished and plushly decorated and every one of them was identical – a bedroom. By pressing switches and turning controls on the panel, the woman at the desk could rotate the central turnable, swinging her class around to face any particular room setting: and also bring the lights up and down.

'The teacher in charge is on a leave of absence from the Montreal fun-girl set-up,' Essex whispered close to the American's ear, keeping his voice low to avoid interrupting the women's commentary. 'The others are from all over. The boys from the Trans-Canadian Service, of course, and the girls from the houses and call apartments.'

The others Essex referred to were the demonstrator teachers. Spagnoli made a quick count of twenty room settings and each of these was occupied by a handsome young man and a beautiful girl. All except one such couple sat patiently waiting on the side of the bed in their respective bedroom mock-up, the lights out. The bedroom into which the class looked was brilliantly lit. The girl who was on view was completely naked, her firm, evenly tanned body spread-eagled across the bed. The man was dressed in the lower half of a scuba diver's wetsuit with a hole cut to expose his genitals. He was kneeling on the bed between the girl's parted thighs.

'Many men make the mistake of thinking they are the only sex to have fetishes,' the woman at the desk was explaining. 'This is totally wrong. Women, too, may experience a heightening of sexual enjoyment from the texture of rubber, leather, plastic, etcetera.'

As she spoke, the couple on the starkly lighted bed demonstrated. The man grasped the woman's ankles and lifted her legs, massaging the calves against his rubber encased thighs. Then he eased one knee forward, so that her thigh came into contact with his.

'But, as we always stress, it must be the woman who encourages the use of aids to sexual stimulation. One woman's fetish is likely to be another's turn-off.'

Spagnoli looked at the scene with bulging eyes, and felt certain the girl on the bed was not faking her passion when the rubber-encased knee nudged her gaping sex. There was no doubt about the man's lust. He was rigidly ready to enter his partner, and he did so – a moment before the demonstration was plunged into darkness and the turnable swung a few degrees.

'Good, Angelo?' Essex asked softly, wishing he could derive some kind of lift from watching exhibitions of heterosexual acts. It might help to keep thoughts of John Stark at bay. But he couldn't. He didn't feel the revulsion which Swenson experienced. He merely looked and felt nothing. Not even the sight of a naked young man could stir him when there was an equally unclad woman nearby.

'Tremendous!' Spagnoli muttered, and caught his breath as the next bedroom mock-up was lit.

This time it was the man who was totally naked. Supine on the bed and held there by bounds at his ankles and wrists. A beautiful blonde teenager stood at the side of the bed, wearing white ankle socks and a diaper.

'The distaste of making love to a fat matron may not be all you have to suffer,' the woman at the desk announced flatly. 'Flagellation is becoming increasingly popular in our particular segment of the market. Understandably, perhaps, divorcees who have experienced marriage breakdown because of a husband's harsh treatment are the women most likely to request this. There is, of course, an extra charge.'

The woman at the side of the bed stooped down and picked up a leather thong with a bone handle. With a squeal of delight, she lashed the whip across the stomach of the helpless man. His scream of pain was as genuine as the red weals left by the thong.

The woman at the desk raised her voice to be heard above the sound of pain. 'Whenever we know a woman has these tastes – mostly because she is an old customer – we supply her with an escort who has volunteered since he shares the same desires.' She switched out the lights and turned the class towards another mock-up. 'The manner of dress chosen by the woman is, of course, immaterial. The baby costume was simply an example.'

Essex was watching Spagnoli closely and saw, as the next demonstration was illuminated, that the example of the sixty-nine position was an anti-climax to him following the flag scene.

'Enough for now, Angelo?' he asked softly. 'Don't worry about it. Even the pupils get a little jaded before they've made a half circuit of the room.'

Spagnoli nodded, looking a little shattered for the first time since Essex had met him. He sucked in a deep breath of air once the door had closed on the sex-permeated room. 'Jesus, Rick,' he gasped. 'I can't wait to get back across the border and get something like this started.'

'You think you can get the recruits?' Essex asked, steering the American towards the end of the corridor. 'Remember, what you've seen tonight is just the training. When those guys start earning back the investment we've made in them, it won't be beautiful pieces of young nooky they'll be sharing the real bedrooms with.'

'You got them, and we'll get them,' Spagnoli answered enthusiastically, regaining his lost energy. 'And if they can come back to a place like this every three months – hell, I figure we can get some guys without paying them.'

A door at the end led into a narrower passage which was, in fact, a covered walkway across a thirty-foot-wide ravine.

Snowflakes, swirled by a biting, eddying wind, flurried frantically outside the windows against a backdrop of the pitch black night.

'You could be right,' Essex agreed, pushing open a door on the far side of the walkway and ushering his guest through.

Spagnoli had been here before, on the ground floor of a six-storey, hundred-bedroom hotel. They were in the lobby, half of which was occupied by a heated swimming pool. In and around this, the newcomers and old hands on the company's fun girl and boy circuit were letting their hair down. The central section was an open-plan bar area with music and a space for dancing. It, too, was crowded with the company's young set. Beyond was the reception desk, stairway and elevators to the upper floors. One entire wall of the long, high-ceilinged room was of plate glass. By day or night, providing the weather was fine, the view was breath-taking. Across the skating rink and nursery slopes in the foreground to the ski and sled runs and the high ski jump beyond: the whole man-made complex set against a magnificent natural backdrop of the snow-mantled peaks of the Sharktooth Mountains. But tonight the moon was obscured by low, scudding clouds and the wind-gusted snowflakes of the storm completely blocked the view.

Essex looked sourly at the white-streaked blackness pressing against the glass. Charlie certainly wouldn't be able to fly up to Snowy Ridge in this weather. And if the storm was also raging at lower altitudes the road up from the Alaska Highway was surely blocked – maybe even the main route, as well.

'The bar on the top floor is usually quieter than this, Angelo,' he said, brightening as the thought struck him that, if Charlie couldn't make it through the weather, then neither could Stark. 'Or I can have something sent up to my suite?'

Spagnoli shook his head as he followed Essex along the edge of the pool. Both men received a flashing smile from every youngster. 'I've seen them at work, Rick. Like to watch them at play for a while.'

'Sure,' Essex agreed, steering his guest towards two vacant barstools. The hi-fi was oozing out something soft and sentimental for the couples clinging to each other and moving slowly around the dance floor. The two men could talk without shouting after Essex had ordered a Scotch for himself and a bourbon for Spagnoli.

'They look a pretty friendly bunch,' the American said, ignoring his drink as he swung around on the stool to survey the couples at the tables, on the dancefloor and in and at the edge of the pool.

Essex smiled secretly, aware that his visitor just could not get enough of the sight of so many nubile girls with their firm young bodies and willing eyes. The boys meant nothing to him, which didn't upset Essex. He believed in everyone to their own taste. 'I guess you're not involved in the vice section at present?'

'Protection,' the American replied distastefully. 'And narcotic co-ordination on the Mexican routes. But if I can swing this deal for the West Coast operation, I'll make damn sure I get control of it.'

'Take a drink, Angelo,' Essex invited. 'Then take your pick.'

'You mean . . .?'

'It's one of the fringe benefits. Our fun girl circuit has a career structure just like any other branch of the company. The girls start on the streets, move to the houses and then get to the call apartments if that's the way they shape up. The really good ones, if they've got brains in their heads as well as minds between their legs, can reach executive status. And they know it never does any harm to their careers if they can impress the top brass.'

Spagnoli began to breathe hard, and he twisted around on the stool suddenly. He took a drink. 'The girl in the last classroom we visited, Rick? The one with the whip and the ankle socks?'

'You like her?'

The American's voice became gravelly with anticipation. 'I like what she was doing.'

Essex grinned. 'First pick the girl that appeals to you most. Or more than one if that's your bag. Every fun girl will do whatever you want – and they're all trained to do it right.'

'Wow!' the American exclaimed, sounding like a college boy on the point of making it for the first time in his life. His excited eyes raked the big room again, with a purpose that went beyond mere looking and admiring. They did a double take and then settled on a table where a couple were sipping drinks and watching the dancers. 'The redhead with the big tits and the black dress.'

The couple sensed they were being watched and glanced at the bar. Essex crooked a finger. The girl got up, smoothed the dress over her hips and walked elegantly between the tables. She halted, standing submissively in front of the two men perched on the barstools.

'Something I can do for you, Mr. Essex?' she asked. 'I'm Charmaine.'

'For our guest,' Essex told her.

The American drank in the sight of her lovely face and voluptuous body. He thought she was about eighteen and that her hair colour was natural. His wife and two teenage daughters – just a couple of years younger than this girl – were also redheads. 'And she'll do absolutely anything I want, Rick?'

'Just tell her,' Essex assured.

'What about . . . a . . . props?' Spagnoli wanted to know.

'There's a fully supplied stores in the admin building,' Essex answered. 'Charmaine will draw whatever is needed.'

'And booze?'

'Ring room service.'

Perhaps it was imagination, but Essex thought the boy who had just been relieved of Charmaine's company looked like a younger version of Charlie Swenson. Watching Spagnoli and the girl walking over to the elevators, Essex felt an ache in his lower stomach. He hadn't seen the boy before – he was probably a new recruit, at Snowy Ridge for training. Maybe he could smuggle the boy up to his suite, ball him and then take him out to prevent it getting around he had messed with the help.

But then he shook his head, dismissing the idea. He would wait for Charlie. He went up to his suite, trying to cheer himself with the thought of the two and a half million dollars the Canadian arm would receive in consultant fees if the US syndicate bought the male prostitution circuit idea. That would more than make up for what he had lost by releasing the grip he had on Groves Industries Incorporated.

The telephone rang as he climbed into bed. The lack of a partner to share it with had brought back the black mood to swamp the comfort drawn from thinking about the deal with the syndicate. The call from the vice-president in charge of company operations in Alberta plunged Essex deeper into the slough of depression. The carefully worded report told of three more enforcers dead. And, even worse, Stark was now in western Canada and on the loose.

'We're doing everything we can to locate him, Mr. Essex,' the man in the Edmonton office of the Trans-Canadian Escort Service said after a long silence had greeted his report.

'Make sure you fucking do before he gets to Snowy Ridge!' Essex snarled into the mouthpiece, and slammed the handset on to the cradle. Then he snatched it up again and was about to dial the room service number to order a bottle of Haig Pinch sent to the room.

But, as his finger stabbed angrily into the numbered hole, the bedroom door was flung open. He whirled in the bed, staring at the doorway with terror-wide eyes. Charlie Swenson stepped out of the darkened lounge into the low-lit bedroom. Melted snow saturated his fur-lined parka and pants and his handsome face was blue with cold.

'Surprise, Rick baby!' he yelled, throwing out his arms,

his hands encased in thick mittens. 'Man, have I had problems getting—'

The fear and anxiety shed from Essex like snow off a slope in the first warm sunlight of spring. He tore at the fastenings on his pyjamas. 'I don't want to know how you got here, you beautiful bitch!' he yelled. 'Just so long as you didn't freeze your ass off doing it.'

CHAPTER THIRTEEN

IT was cold in Calgary, but there was no snow or threat of it. The sky was cloudless, with the quarter moon and a million stars gleaming clear and bright. The couple Stark was following had spent a long time looking at the night sky from the interior of the woman's Dodge Challenger parked at Heritage Park. That was after they had eaten a late dinner at a plush restaurant on Seventh Avenue and before they went up Husky Tower to get a panoramic view of the city and the Rocky Mountains. It was after one when they reached the Warner Hotel on Centre Street, parked the car and went up to the woman's room.

After shooting up the Mini, Stark had made good time barrelling the Plymouth south through Alberta. He went through Edmonton without stopping, for although he was certain the city would have an office of Trans-Canadian, it was too close to where he had last hit the company. Calgary was two hundred miles down the freeway. Not exactly the far end of the earth, but maybe the company heat would not be turned so high there.

The one-time cowboy town gone respectable as the administrative centre for the province's oil industry was quietly swinging when Stark rolled the battered Barracuda into the city. He located the office of the Trans-Canadian Escort Service on Eighth Avenue by the simple process of checking for a listing in the telephone directory. But, as he had expected, it was closed up for the night. He had three courses of action opened to him: break into the office, wait for it to open the next morning, or try to spot a couple with the right young male-elderly female mix. He elected this last and, guessing that most of Trans-Canadian's specialist clients were out-of-towners in the city for a visit, he checked the hotel bars. The upmarket, expensive places; for this area of the escort agency's service would come high, aimed at the rich.

He spotted the fat, fifty, bottle-blonde Mrs. Amelia Ritchie in the Warner Hotel's Starlight Lounge Cocktail Bar. He knew her name because she was paged for a long-distance telephone call and had to leave her companion for a few minutes. He was a dark-haired, blue-eyed boy in his early twenties who was six feet tall and not skinny. His manners were impeccable and his attitude to the woman was smoothly attentive. Only while she was away taking her telephone call did he allow his distaste for the assignment to show. He sank two fast double gins without mixers.

Then had come the night on the town, the pleasures a mixture of the simple and the sophisticated, the cheap and the expensive. Because of the couple's ill-matched pairing, Stark was able to maintain a loose tail whenever they left the car, for it was not easy to lose them in a crowd. And, at the end of the sightseeing tour, their return to the Warner Hotel would have seemed to make the tail chore a waste of time. But Stark didn't think of it so. They might have stopped off at a place where he could have braced the man. They had not. But, in addition, Stark had become as certain as he could be that the male prostitute did not have enforcer cover. It wouldn't be standard under normal conditions, but with the Revenger in Canada, protection might have been considered.

'Four-one-five, isn't it, Mrs. Ritchie?' the night man at the reception desk said as the couple approached him. He already had the tagged key in his outstretched hand.

'My friend is coming up for a nightcap,' the over-painted, over-dressed and bejewelled matron replied in an upper-crust English accent. 'Please ask for a magnum of champagne to be delivered to my room.'

'Certainly, Mrs. Ritchie. It'll be a pleasure.'

The clerk was using the telephone before the couple had reached the elevator, working for the tip he hoped to get at the end of the woman's stay in the hotel. Stark stood patiently at the desk and when the room service order had been placed, he used an excuse which had never failed him in the past.

'Single with bath for one night? There was some kind of mix-up with luggage at the airport. My bags are probably on their way to Hong Kong.'

He had his wallet out, showing his willingness to pay in advance. The bar and restaurant off the lobby were closed and darkened. Nobody occupied the comfortable sofas and armchairs spread in front of the desk. Stark had no sense of danger, but stayed discreetly alert anyway, ready to draw the Colt Commander from his waistband if that was the way it had to be.

The clerk was apologetic about accepting advance payment. Stark signed the register as Stanley Abbott, a naturalised Canadian of British birth now living in Ottawa. The business of checking in was completed in less than a minute. He was given a key to a room on the sixth floor. He declined the offer of a bell boy to show him up.

'Hate lifts,' he called over his shoulder as he started up the stairway beside the bank of three elevators.

This meant he didn't have to ride up to the sixth floor and then take the stairs back down to the fourth. As soon as he had turned an angle and was out of sight from the lobby, he began to run, taking the steps at two and three with a single stride. Room four-one-five was a long way down a hallway from the head of the stairs. The service elevator was closer. The light began to flash, showing the car on its way up the shaft, as Stark arrived outside the door to Mrs. Ritchie's room. It was very quiet and he could hear the whirr of the electric motor. It reminded him of a young girl straightening her tights in a lift car a long way from here and a lot of deaths ago. He had the big automatic in his right hand and he used the knuckles of his left to rap on the door.

The Warner Hotel was an old building with thick walls and solid doors. He didn't hear anything from room four-one-five until the lock scraped and the door began to open.

He went in with his left shoulder shoving the door wide and his gun hand pressed against his stomach, barrel aimed into the room.

'Champagne's on its way, mate,' he told the dark-haired boy, who had been sent staggering to the floor by the sprung open door. 'I'm the advance guard.'

He stepped into the room and closed the door as the electric motor clicked to a halt. They had not wasted much time. The man had stripped off to his string singlet and mauve underpants. The woman was already in bed, perhaps completely naked. Stark couldn't tell because she had a sheet pulled up to hold against her throat. Her face, looking even more garishly over-painted in contrast with the virgin whiteness of the sheet, was forming into the lines of terror. Her mouth began to open for a scream.

'Make a sound and I'll blast his balls off, lady!' Stark rasped, altering the aim of the gun. 'Can you stand the scandal back home?'

The vivid red mouth snapped closed. The man remained flat on the floor, as if the Colt had an invisible extension which pinned him there. Knuckles rapped on the door.

'Room service, Mrs. Ritchie.'

'I'll go!' the woman said hoarsely.

She got out of bed and she wasn't naked. Just from the waist up, her over-burdened breasts swinging down to stroke her bulging belly as she hurriedly draped a dressing gown over her shoulders. She wore ridiculously small black briefs of the kind that are advertised in the Sunday newspapers and girlie magazines. They had a hole cut out of the crotch. She also wore stockings held up her blue-veined thighs by a pink suspender belt.

'Sexy!' Stark rasped in mock passion as the woman waddled towards the door, belting the gown around her. He brandished the gun and the man rolled over on to all fours and scrambled to a side of the room.

Mrs. Ritchie cracked open the door. 'Never mind the tray,' she said, reached through the crack and hauled in the bottle. Ice clinked against the bucket. She closed the door, then looked ready to sag against it. But suddenly she whirled, anger making her face uglier than ever. Her blazing eyes swung from her escort to Stark and back again. 'What is the meaning of this?' she demanded. 'If it's some kind of blackmail, I'm warning you I—'

'I don't know this guy!' her escort forced around a lump in his throat. 'I swear it . . . unless . . .' His fear heightened. 'Unless it's . . .'

'You've hit it, mate,' Stark told him, and jerked a thumb towards the bed. 'Get back in, lady.'

'This is a nightmare!' Mrs. Ritchie exclaimed. 'You're English, aren't you?'

'As roast beef and Yorkshire pudding,' Stark answered.

The woman swallowed hard. 'I have money. I'll pay anything within reason.'

Stark nodded, 'You're dealing with a reasonable man, darling. Get back into bed and I won't tell the Sunday papers about you, Amelia. Keep the dressing gown on. Another peek at that sexy get up and I might forget what I came here for.'

'Jeremy?' she pleaded in a wailing tone.

'You'd better do as he says, ma'am,' the man urged, still struggling to overcome his fear.

He was small fry in the company. But like every other cog, large and small, in the evil machine of international crime, Jeremy would have heard about Stark. And none of it good. This was something which almost always acted to Stark's advantage. For, as in this case, a company man's fear was compounded of two elements – the presence of the Revenger and the reputation which had preceded that presence.

Stark always endeavoured to avoid hurting innocent parties in his war against the company. But sometimes it was not possible. However, innocence is relative. As Mrs. Ritchie waddled past him to get to the bed, Stark lashed sideways with his gun arm. The underside of the Colt's barrel cracked into the woman's temple. She stopped abruptly, and sighed as her eyes swivelled up in their sockets before the lids dropped. She crumpled to the floor, dropping the champagne bottle. Even before she became still, the dressing gown gaping open to expose her farcically erotic underwear from belly to feet, the automatic had swung back to cover Jeremy. He had moved only to the extent of pressing himself hard against the wall. Stark felt only a minor twinge of regret. The ugly, pathetic old woman had availed herself of a company service. Without her and countless millions like her who sought illicit gratifications for the whole gamut of the darker human wants, the company would not exist.

'Perhaps she'll wake up and think the whole thing really was a nightmare,' Stark said. 'And perhaps you'll still be around to console her with a dream come true.'

'What do you want, Stark?' He tried to sound tough, but his voice came out squeaky. There was just a trace of hardness in his mouthline and he generated a little anger into his eyes as they challenged Stark's easy gaze.

'The name of your boss and the place where he pulls the strings from.'

'I work for the Trans-Canadian Escort Service. The office is on Eighth Avenue. The manager's name is Mr. Campbell.'

'Good start, Jeremy,' Stark congratulated wryly, backing away from the man against the wall. He stooped and picked up the champagne bottle. It was still wet with frosting from the ice bucket. 'You aren't pretending you don't know who I am and what you are. But I haven't been following you and your ladyfriend all night to go on a refresher course. I need some new knowledge.' He glanced around the spacious, tastefully furnished room, then waved the bottle. 'You look the kind of bloke who thinks best when he's lying down.'

Jeremy hesitated, then had to push himself away from the wall. He walked lithely to the bed and sat delicately on its edge, facing Stark. Stark brandished the gun this time, and the man swung up his legs and leaned back, resting his head on the pillow. He interlocked his fingers over his stomach.

Stark was holding the bottle by its neck. He brought it down hard against the bedhead table and it shattered. Champagne frothed. Jeremy shuddered and became rigid. The subdued lighting from the bedhead lamps and the overhead fixtures glinted on the jagged edges of glass growing from the neck of the bottle clasped in Stark's fist. A tear squeezed from the corner of one of Jeremy's suddenly dull blue eyes.

'Something else does the work, mate,' Stark said softly, 'but it's your face that's your fortune.'

Stark leaned down over the rigid man – and knew he'd been had. He had seen from the start that Jeremy had more than a strong stomach. That was to keep him from throwing up when he was in close contact with grotesque old hags like Amelia Ritchie. Stripped down to his underwear it was obvious he commanded a great deal of physical strength. Now he proved he had the fast reflexes to use it to good purpose.

He was scared, but the single tear was a fake and the rigid posture of his body was a preparation for action rather than submission. As Stark's hands drew near, hovering, Jeremy quite literally sprang into a fast counter-move. His hands went into action first, jerking apart and shooting upwards. At the moment they fastened around Stark's wrists, his back curled up off the bed. Stark was pulled down towards him and his jaw smashed into the top of the man's skull.

Pain shot through Stark's head, freezing his facial muscles. The room went dark on him for a moment. 'Bastard!' he hissed through teeth which were clenched and aching as if every one was decayed.

Then Jeremy bit him: just as Stark's vision recovered and he prepared to power backwards, forcing the man to release him or follow the roll. Jeremy simply turned his head to the side, swung it towards Stark's gun hand and sank his teeth into the pad of flesh beneath the base of the thumb.

Pain was vented in a grunt and Stark splayed his injured hand. The big automatic dropped to the bed between Jeremy's thighs. Jeremy's jaws opened and he pulled his head away. Blood coated his lips and he spat it out. More blood spurted from Stark's hand. Jeremy released the wrist of the injured hand and tried for the gun instead of a punch. It was a mistake, but he didn't realise it as his hand fisted around the butt of the Colt. He even emitted a squeal of delight as he dragged the gun up off the bed.

Stark brought across his free hand and gave a flick of his wrist. Blood splashed from the bite wound and spattered into Jeremy's eyes. Revulsion, rather than partial and temporary blindness, caused Jeremy to release his grip on Stark's wrist and fist the warm, sticky liquid from his eyes. Stark stabbed with the neck of the bottle. Jagged edges of green glass punctured Jeremy's gun arm midway between the wrist and elbow. He tried to ride with the stab, going sideways and pushing his forearm against the bed. Stark went with him all the way. The glass sank deeper into the flesh and scraped against bone. Blood oozed from the holes, trickled down the curves of the arm and expanded into crimson stains across the white quilt. The fingers uncurled from around the butt of the gun, but Jeremy still had an uninjured arm with a free hand. He whipped it away from his blood-stained eyes and made a stiff-fingered stab towards Stark's eyes.

Stark lunged to the side and dragged the bottle after him. His free hand, still scattering droplets of blood, clamped over Jeremy's mouth. He felt the man's hot breath against his palm, but the scream was trapped inside. Blood poured in torrents from the long gouges made by the broken bottle – bone-deep furrows in the flesh from mid forearm to shoulder. Jeremy's bulging eyes swivelled down to look across Stark's clamped hand at the massive lacerations in his own arm. There wasn't time for the loss of blood to have effected him. So it was the mere sight of the awesome injury that drained the strength out of him. He remained conscious, but his body went limp. Stark took no chances. His actions were fast and fluid. He released his grip over the man's lower face, scooped up the gun and sprang back from the bed. But Jeremy's attitude of fear-aroused weakness was no fake. He lay utterly still, staring at the raw meat of his ripped arm.

'I'm maimed for life,' he gasped, reaching across with his good arm and touching his fingers to the blood.

Stark leaned over him again: faster this time. He rested the broken bottle against the man's pulsing throat and jabbed the Colt muzzle into his stomach. 'I can help you out, mate!' he rasped. 'Make it a short life.'

'No!' Jeremy begged.

'So teach me what I came to learn, old son,' Stark urged.

'Rick Essex is the man you want,' Jeremy blubbered and Stark eased up on the pressure with the bottle. The man's throat moved frantically when he blurted out the words. 'Christ, I can't feel my arm.'

'It's still there,' Stark told him wryly. 'Where will I find him?'

'I don't know! He could be anywhere. He moves around all the time.'

'So where's company headquarters?'

'There isn't one.'

The gun muzzle pressed harder against his stomach.

'Not just one. Each province has its own. Essex moves around. The front operation's called Essex Leisure Limited. There are offices all over. Please, Stark. I've got to reach a doctor. I'll bleed to death.'

Stark halfway believed the man. Jeremy was so frightened he did not even realise the basic fact that Stark could not allow him to remain alive.

'One last chance, mate.'

He expected a contorted expression of anguish and a blubbering denial of further knowledge. But, instead, a look of relief flooded the handsome features and there was excitement in Jeremy's tone. 'Wait! There was some talk at the agency office this afternoon. Essex has got a visitor from the States. They met in Edmonton. The Yank wants to look over the Trans-Canadian operation. Essex is sure to take him up to Snowy Ridge.'

'Where's that?'

Jeremy was looking up at Stark with a plea for deliverance fighting its way through the pain in his eyes. 'Sharktooth Range west of Fort Nelson. Northern British Columbia. Please, Stark. I'll fix up a doctor. Just beat it out of here. I won't say nothing. If I did, my life wouldn't be worth two cents.'

'That's over-priced,' Stark said. 'And I never buy when I can take something for nothing.'

He lifted the gun away from the man's stomach, then drove it downwards again: hard and fast. And lower. A groan of agony ripped from Jeremy's lips. He had too much pain to worry about the jagged edges of glass as he rolled on to his side and doubled-up. Stark had jerked away the broken bottle anyway. He dropped it to the floor. Then his gun hand rose and fell again. The butt of the Colt smashed into Jeremy's temple and the punished man became still and silent: except for the gentle movements and sounds of his breathing.

Soon, even these were ended as Jeremy died without regaining consciousness. The method was simple – a pillow held firmly over his mouth and nostrils. Then Stark went into the bathroom and discovered that an appetite for the driving bodies of young men was not Amelia Ritchie's only vice. She was also a hypochondriac. He had a lot of trouble finding some aspirin among the many bottles of pills and tonics in the cabinet and on the shelves and window ledge. He swallowed two, more in hope than faith that they would ease the pain attacking his jaw muscles and gums. He also found some sticking plaster, gauze and a tube of Savlon. He dressed the ugly looking bite on his hand and returned to the bedroom.

Jeremy remained inert on the bed. The woman on the floor was snoring. She had a whole set of matched luggage in the bottom of the walk-in wardrobe. Dark blue and made of fibreglass. He took the largest case. It was empty. Crossing to the door, he flipped the skirts of the dressing gown to conceal Mrs. Ritchie's obscene stomach and thighs.

'You're a big girl now,' he muttered and let himself out of the room, reaching back inside to switch off the lights before closing the self-locking door behind him.

He used the stairs again, halting at the angle on the last flight to look down into the lobby. It's sole occupant was the night clerk behind the desk. The man looked at Stark in surprise as he descended the stairs and approached the desk. Stark winked at him.

'It was a con, mate,' he said. 'There was a lady I knew would fall for me and I guessed you'd have a house rule against it.'

The desk clerk blinked and swallowed hard.

'Keep the money for your co-operation.' He put the key on the desk. 'I didn't use the room.'

'What you got in the case?' He edged closer to the telephone.

Stark snapped open the catches and displayed the fact that the case was empty. 'I could buy one cheaper than a night's charge in this place,' he pointed out.

'Okay, beat it!' the clerk said, annoyed. 'But don't try it again. This is a class place. I could lose my job.'

'Cheers,' Stark said, closing the case, moving towards the door and raising a hand in farewell.

'Hey?'

He stopped and turned around. 'What?'

'What happened to your hand?'

Stark looked at the inexpert dressing on the base of his thumb. He grinned. 'Somebody put the bite on me. But it wasn't me who got chewed up.'

CHAPTER FOURTEEN

'HI, you must be one of the new ones. I'm Goldy. I've never been laid in the snow.'

She was five feet nothing, but a lot of woman had been packed into the small bundle. Even muffled up in an all-in-one fur-lined snowsuit the generous curves of her body could be seen. She had dark brown hair, strands of which had squeezed out from under the hood. Her face seemed to be that of an ingenuous girl of eighteen or so: at first glance. But the green eyes demanded a second, longer look. And they seemed as old as womankind. Or perhaps, Stark thought, he was just over-reacting to the girl's opening remark.

'You'd either go cold or the snow would start to steam,' he answered.

'Fantastic!' Goldy squealed and tugged on the ring at her throat.

The vivid red snowsuit was unzipped all the way to her crotch in a single, swift movement and Stark saw why it displayed the lines of her body so well. She wore nothing underneath. There were press-studs at the wrist and when she had unfastened these, a shrug of her shoulders sent the suit into a shapeless heap around her ankles. Her hair was richly coloured and very long. It grew only on her head. Her big breasted, narrow-waisted, broad-hipped body was richly coloured and exquisitely short. She had no hirsute triangle at the base of her flat belly and the shaven area was as evenly tanned as the rest of her.

'Hey, you really are a new boy, aren't you?' she asked. She stooped down, delved her hands under the snowsuit and worked on the ankle press-studs. When they popped, she stepped delicately out of the suit. Now she wore only blue and red, canvas and rubber sneakers.

And Stark wore a new expression. The look of awed surprise had gone and been replaced by an eager grin.

'A live one at last!' Goldy squealed in heightened delight, then screamed as she sat down in the snow. It's coldness against her buttocks and the undersides of her legs took her breath away for a moment. Then she threw herself down at full stretch and began to roll back and forth. Laughter trilled from her wide mouth as every part of her compact, firmly curved body and face was invigorated by the snow. 'Come on!' she challenged. 'Let's motor, baby!'

She was on her back, legs splayed and arms spread wide. The dark brown nipples probed skywards from the crests of her breasts and her sex gaped. Goose bumps added new curves to her honey-toned flesh displayed against the dazzling whiteness of the sun-sparkled snow.

'I'll be back, darling,' Stark told her, and stepped behind the rock from where he had emerged to first see the girl.

'Hey, where you going?' she called, a hint of annoyance in her tone.

'I'm shy,' Stark answered, shedding the sheepskin coat he had bought in Trutch on his long, fast drive up the Alaska Highway. 'Got this thing about undressing in front of women.'

Goldy laughed. 'We'll sure cure you of that phobia up here.'

Under the topcoat he still wore the business suit and other clothes Groves had bought for him in Stockholm. They made him stand out like a sore thumb on the white-covered, tree-scattered slopes beneath Snowy Ridge. He draped each garment across the suitcase and when he was naked, he stepped out. His tall, hard-skinned body towered over the submissively postured girl and she gave a whistle of admiration.

'New, and ready, willing and able,' she breathed, her eyes raking him from head to toe. Then they settled on a central point. She was shivering and there was a blue tint to the tan now. 'Plug me in and turn me on, man,' she demanded.

The air temperature was pleasant, even against his naked flesh: he could feel the warmth of the noon sun on his shoulders. But, as he dropped to his knees between her parted, trembling thighs, a biting cold gripped him. In a moment, the radical change in temperature might have made him useless to the girl. But, before that moment was gone, he had lowered himself on to her and sunk the most vulnerable part of his body into the gripping warmth of her.

'Man, that's good!' she sighed, swinging up her legs to lock her feet at the small of his back.

Stark had had to do a lot of back-tracking last night. Two hundred miles up the freeway to Edmonton. Then out on the road to Capitan before the swing westwards beyond Lesser Slave Lake. Night ended and morning began while he slept in the car parked off the road between Grand Prairie and Dawson Creek. Three hundred miles from Edmonton as the crow flies, but Stark wasn't a crow.

The bird beneath him was getting warmer. Each drew from the other's body heat as he drove into her and she thrust against him. He cupped the back of her head, pressing her face against his chest. Her tongue darted and her teeth nipped.

There had been just two hours sleep before he started out again. He was in the mountains then, with snow banked on the high slopes. The further north he went, the closer the road came to the snow. And then, at Pink Mountain, he was on it and he bought a set of wheel chains from a service station in the town.

The girl's hands were constantly moving. Playing in his hair, trailing against his neck and clawing at his neck. Moans of ecstatic pleasure escaped her lips between each sucking bite.

The ploughs had been out to open the highway in the early morning and there was no threat of new snow from the clear, cobalt blueness of the sky. He swayed a little and his eyes threatened to close while the man who ran the clothing store at Trutch showed him coats. But, back behind the wheel, the exhaustion retreated. He kept the window rolled down and protected his eyes with dark glasses.

Goldy's moans became high-pitched. Her clawed hands raked harder over his back and she forced more strength into her clinging legs. Her nipples seemed to have a metallic rigidity against his flesh. The sweat of passion adhered the skin of her belly to his.

Snowy Ridge was signposted at intervals along a winding, tarmacked road that rose through the mountains at a constantly steep gradient. But each sign bore the warning: PRIVATE – ADMITTANCE BY INVITATION ONLY. When the posted distance to his destination had come down to a mile, he stopped the car. He used the fallen branch of a tree to probe a snowdrift at the side of the road. The ground beneath it was level and it didn't cover anything solid. He got back into the car, manoeuvred it until it straddled the road, then pressed the accelerator to the floor with the gears in reverse. The entire rear half of the car was buried before the weight of snow called a halt. He had been prepared to smash the windscreen to get out, but it didn't prove necessary. He was able to open the door and pull out the heavy suitcase. But it meant he had to spend a lot of the time piling snow around and over the top of the exposed section of the Plymouth. He marked the hiding place with the tree branch before setting off on foot for Snowy Ridge.

'Fantastic!' Goldy shrieked, and shuddered into orgasm.

Stark was drained an instant later and the sweat between their flesh seemed to turn to ice as the girl became limp and exhaustion threatened to plunge him into euphoric sleep.

'It's got skiing beats hand down as my favourite winter sport,' he muttered, burying his face in her freshly perfumed hair.

'You're suffocating me!' she warned in a muffled voice.

Stark contemplated the act.

He had stopped the car with only a few hundred yards to spare. For the marked distances applied to the Snowy Ridge Hotel and its adjacent buildings. Had he driven blithely around the next bend at the top of a rise, upwards of fifty pairs of eyes might have seen him. On foot, he was able to dive into the cover of a group of rocks when he spotted the danger.

He was looking down the slope of a shallow valley, towards the side of the hotel, its windows glinting in the warm sunlight. This slope, at one side of the road, served as a nursery run for novice skiers. There were a dozen of them on it, practising basic moves in the open and among the widely spaced pine, fir and spruce trees. A handful of brightly garbed men and women were on the ice-rink in front of the hotel. But the majority of those out enjoying the exclusive pleasures of the sunlit snow were on the steeper slope of the valley's curving far side. Hissing down the race course, spraying through the slalom, powering off the ski-jump, roaring along the sled-run. And when, in every case, they reached the broad apron of level snow spread before the hotel and rink, they climbed aboard the chair-lift to be carried high up the slope again.

He eased up, away from and out of the girl.

'Man, there sure isn't anything we can teach you about shafting a woman,' Goldy said breathlessly.

'I've done it before,' Stark told her. He began to shiver then, and moved towards the largest of the group of rocks into which he had dived at the top of the rise. From this side a stand of timber hid him and the girl from the people on the slopes and floor of the valley.

'I don't care that you can't stand being watched when you dress,' Goldy called to him as he started to clothe his chilled body. 'That never is any fun.'

As he stepped from behind the rock, intent on making the group of trees, the girl had strolled out of the timber. Luckily, he had been able to drop the suitcase before she saw it. Its weight sunk it half into the snow: it was heavy with the A-R 18, the Savage sporting rifle, cartons and magazines of shells and a pack of high explosive. The Combat Magnums he carried on him – one in his waistband and the other in a pocket of the topcoat.

After Goldy's opening comment had hit him like a verbal thunderbolt, Stark had recovered quickly. Snowy Ridge was the headquarters of the Canadian company's male prostitution circuit. Sex was the name of the high-paying game and Stark was not about to turn down a free sample. The short exchanges before and after the unorthodox but very enjoyable ball in the snow had told him the winter sports resort was not merely a front for the administration of the circuit. The young men came here to learn their specialised trade – and Goldy had mistaken him for a pupil. He decided it would serve his purpose to allow her to live as long as she failed to see any holes in the pretence.

He left the suitcase where it was as he stepped out from the rock again. She was back inside the zippered snowsuit, looking cuddly and strangely innocent.

'That was the best yet since I've been up here this time,' she told him enthusiastically. 'So far I've been with the refresher guys and for them the novelty's worn off.' She giggled. 'Sometimes it feels like something else has worn off.'

'Pleasure to have been of service,' Stark answered.

'You walk up?'

He nodded.

'Pleasure was half mine, sweetie. Now I'll give you an easier ride.' She swung around and trudged through the churned up snow into the trees.

Stark hesitated a moment, then followed her. The spot where he had gained his practical introduction to one aspect of life at Snowy Ridge was clearly defined. He hadn't noticed any steam rising, but the impression of Goldy's body was left deep in the snow. In the trees was a motorised four-seater sled with runners at the front and spiked wheels at the rear.

'Hop in,' she invited.

He did, taking the seat at the front beside her and turning up the collar of his coat. The exhaust fumes from the engine tainted the pine-fresh air until she had driven the sled clear of the timber. But, when they were on the open slope, pointed downhill, she cut off the sound and pulled a lever to raise the wheels. The runners made a pleasant hissing sound sliding over the snow.

'Tell me something?' Stark said, his narrowed eyes surveying the scene below through the dark lenses of the sunglasses.

'Gee, isn't this great?' she trilled. 'What?' She began to spin the steering wheel one way and then the other, taking a snaking course down the hill.

'Why's your name Goldy?'

'It's really Penelope, would you believe,' she said happily. 'But at the Winnipeg house where I work they say I'm worth my weight in gold. I get more repeat clients than any other girl there.'

'Yeah, I would believe,' Stark told her: liking her, but as ready to kill her as he had been a few moments ago. The fun girls were as liable to die at his hands as enforcers, executives, undertakers or anybody else who worked for the company.

She steered the sled on a skirting course around the nursery slope area and on level ground used the engine again.

'Guess we could both use a hot shower, uh?' she asked as she drove the sled expertly around the skating rink and halted it at the end of a line of similar vehicles parked outside the hotel entrance. She jumped out and started up the steps swept clear of snow. 'See you around, man,' she called back. 'Maybe we'll get together again, in a class maybe?'

'I'll try to remember to bring an apple,' he answered, but she was entering the hotel lobby and he only spoke softly.

The large number of people around was to Stark's advantage as he climbed wearily from the sled, regretting what had happened up at the top of the slope. It had been good, but energy-draining. And he didn't have too much of that to spare. He didn't follow the girl up the steps and through the glass doors in the glass wall. There were a lot of people in the bar and around the pool. Maybe as many as there were outside. But he didn't want to push his luck. Although the size of the group meant that a lot of people were strangers to a lot of others: it also multiplied the chances of somebody spotting him as a hardened, more experienced version of the John Stark whose prison photograph had been seen by every company employee and outside contact in the world.

Outside, he could keep his coat collar turned high and the dark glasses over his eyes to reduce this danger. But he had to get some sleep. It didn't take a lot out of a man to squeeze the trigger of a gun. But he needed an unfuzzed brain to find his quarry without arousing suspicion, and then the strength and speed to get away before the crap hit the fan afterwards.

He moved along in front of the hotel, aware of the high standard of beauty of the women and the good looks of the men. And the bursting youth of all of them. This told him that the executives who ran the company's Canadian arm had apparently not thought it necessary to bring the enforcers up to Snowy Ridge. It also made him wonder how the little sex-bomb in the red snowsuit had mistaken him for a new recruit to the handsome and youthful elite. Weariness made him feel middle-aged and used-up.

He tramped past the start of the narrow ravine which cut deeply into the earth between the hotel and the long, low building stretched out to one side. This building, which had a double doorway at each end, looked deserted and there was no noise coming from it. The nearest door swung open easily when he pushed it and he went inside. The wall of heat into which he walked made him realise just how cold he had got during the aftermath of the crazy sex in the snow. And the warmer he became, moving cautiously along the broad corridor, the more weary he felt.

He opened several doors and discovered a classroom-like set-up behind each of them. Because of what Goldy had said to him and what he had seen so far, he was only mildly surprised when he looked into the room with the central turnable and the partitioned areas around the sides.

'I am your slave and I have been naughty,' Angelo

Spagnoli said. 'You must punish me, Charmaine. With your hands first. Then the hair brush.'

There were no lights on in the big room. Just natural daylight filtering in through cracks in the drape curtains pulled across the windows. Stark's pleasure at seeing so many comfortable-looking beds was abruptly wiped out by the sound of the man's voice: patently not the voice of a young man. He slid into the room, closed the door silently behind him and delved a hand into his pocket to curl it around the butt of the Magnum.

'You must tell me if I hurt you too much, Angelo,' the red-headed fun girl replied.

Stark had them pin-pointed – in one of the bedroom mock-ups which was only partially visible from the door. He went to the side, moving into and out of the room settings.

'But I want to feel pain, my beautiful young mistress,' the American syndicate man pleaded.

There was a crack as a hand smacked hard on to naked flesh.

'You have been a very naughty boy,' the girl chided. 'I will smack you and smack you and smack you.'

More cracks, each louder than the last. The man began to sob like a child.

Stark had had enough. As he peered around the end of the partition and looked towards the bed being used by the American syndicate man and the company fun girl, he felt physically sick. And the nausea which he had to force back down his throat into his stomach seemed to trigger a strange revitalisation through his weary body and mind. He was sick of perverted sex. He recalled the childhood fantasy he had brought to life with Belinda Jarratt; the obscene old lady in the Calgary hotel room; the way he had emptied his lust into the willing body of an innocent-looking girl named Goldy who was a whore. And he had to make a physical effort to prevent his imagination from running images of the kind of lessons that were taught and learned in this room.

Angelo Spagnoli and Charmaine were not part of an imaginary vision. He was real, lying naked and face down on the bed, wrists and ankles lashed to each corner. And so was she, dressed in a clear plastic raincoat, black stockings, high-heeled shoes, glassless spectacles and nothing else: her hand rising and then falling hard to crash against the man's buttocks.

The obscene tableau of sex being dragged through the dirt was like a crystallisation of all the company's evil. A beautiful young girl had been corrupted to such an extent that she entered willingly and eagerly into the spirit of gratifying the twisted needs of the degenerate who was exhorting her to greater violence. As she snatched up a hairbrush and began to lash at the man's reddening flesh with it, Stark knew that far more diabolical perversions had taken place in this room. But to watch this was enough,when it was allied with the empty sensation in the pit of his stomach – reminding him of what he had done to Goldy, a whore who was as skilled as this one in the arts of the darker side of sex.

Stark felt the urge to kill sweep through him in the wake of the receding nausea. And he knew he wouldn't be able to fight it back with the suddenly less pressing need to sleep. He stepped out from behind the partition and jerked the Magnum from his pocket. The girl was wacking the man's buttocks, using the edge of the brush and drawing blood. Much more blood spurted from her: bursting from the massive exit hole in the top of her head. He had simply pressed the muzzle of the Magnum against her ear and squeezed the trigger. As she turned, the smile of pleasure dying to be replaced by an expression of depthless horror, his hand slid off the slippery surface of the coat at her shoulder and altered the angle of entry.

The report was loud, cutting across and silencing Spagnoli's howls of pleasurable pain. The American became rigid and craned his head around to look sideways at Stark. He shuddered as the dead body of the girl slumped across him. The man's looks backed up the evidence of his voice. He was no clean-limbed youngster come to Snowy Ridge to learn how to satisfy the lusts of rich old women.

'Who . . . what . . . ?' The American could say no more. Stark had moved to the head of the bed and squatted down, showing Spagnoli the killer look in his ice-cold blue eyes. He rested the muzzle of the Magnum against the tip of Spagnoli's nose.

'I ask the questions, mate,' he said softly. 'Where's Rick Essex?'

The American tried to draw away, but his bonds limited movement. The gun muzzle, stinking of burnt cordite, stayed firmly in place.

'I don't know,' the American managed to squeeze around the solid wedge of fear driven into his throat. 'Around here someplace.'

'Describe him.'

Spagnoli did, his voice hoarse, as if he were being strangled by his own terror. He used words of one syllable with long spaces between them. 'You're Stark, aren't you?' he said when he had finished the description. 'Look, I'm not with the company.'

'Who are you?'

'Angelo Spagnoli. American. With a different organisation.'

Stark nodded. 'I was told about you, mate. The visiting fireman.'

'You don't want to harm me. I'm nothing to do with this outfit.'

Stark gave him a contemptuous look and stood up. 'Different name, but the same rotten game,' he said.

He saw where their clothes were piled on the floor, hurriedly discarded. Nearby was a polythene bag. The black stockings and plastic raincoat had been in it. It was printed with a notice: RETURN TO STORES AFTER USE. Spagnoli watched Stark with horrified fascination as he picked up the bag and pulled off his necktie.

'What . . . what are you . . . going to do?'

'Show how adaptable I am,' Stark answered. 'Hold still.'

Spagnoli didn't. He began to yell for help and to rock his head back and forth between his outstretched arms. But he didn't have a chance. The polythene encased his head and within moments the tie was knotted tightly around his neck. He continued to throw his head from side to side and to yank at his bonds as the clear plastic film became cloudy with his expelled breath. And then there was only his own used air to suck in again.

'Relax and enjoy it, mate,' Stark muttered as he retreated from the stage set bedroom. 'I thought suffering was your bag.'

The American's muted shouts and choked breathing had ended before Stark reached the door. He cracked it first, and checked that the corridor was empty before stepping outside. The double killing had revitalised him still further after revulsion had triggered the energy-giving hate. But he knew it was a phoney sensation – that exhaustion could hit him with the suddenness and power of a sledgehammer at any time.

At the exit doors, he halted and surveyed the scene outside. It was much the same as before. The beautiful young girls and the virile young men continued to disport themselves on the ice and the snow. Its virgin whiteness, emphasised by the bright sunlight, was a mocking agent that in Stark's revenge-thirsty mind acted to expand the evil behind the beauty.

He pulled open one of the doors and strolled outside. It was obvious that there was no school today. He wondered if it was Sunday. It was easy to lose track of the passing of time when a mind ran on a single track, oblivious to all else. He felt detached as he ambled through the snow towards the parked sleds – recklessly invulnerable. With a hand fisted around the butt of the Magnum in his pocket he experienced a sensation of incredible power.

Nobody paid any attention to him as he climbed into one

of the sleds. He had trouble starting the cold engine, but when it fired, it settled down to run sweetly. The spiked wheels dug powerfully into the snow and he chugged away from the hotel. The top speed was no more than ten miles an hour on the flat. When the slope began it dropped to half that. He steered in a wide half circle around the ski practice area. Still nobody paid any attention to him.

He was halfway up the slope when a hooter sounded. A glance over his shoulder showed that suddenly he was the only person at Snowy Ridge heading away from the hotel. Everyone else was going downhill. He got ready to abandon the sled and race up into the trees on foot. But the hooter was not a warning to signal that the bodies of Spagnoli and Charmaine had been discovered. There was no sense of urgency in the way the people converged on the hotel.

He drove the sled into the trees and through them, not cutting the engine until he had rounded the rocks. Lifting the suitcase on to the rear seats was the first act of physical strength which had been required since he had retreated from the brink of exhaustion. It proved to him how dead-beat he was. He started the engine again and drove in a circle to re-enter the timber. At the edge of the grove, where he had a panoramic view across the valley, he parked the vehicle, with the spiked wheels lowered to hold it. He opened the suitcase and took out the Savage. He sat in the snow to fit the barrel to the stock and the telescopic sight to the barrel. The Japanese automatic rifle was easier to prepare. All he had to do was unfold the stock and lock it in place. Then he stretched out full-length, focussed the lenses in the telescopic sight and looked through them.

He saw a section of the hotel's façade in narrow-angled magnification. Almost everyone was down from the slopes now, crowding in through the plate glass doors. The faces he saw in close-up all looked happy. And something else? He couldn't pin it down for some time. Then he had it. They looked hungry, too. The hooter had been sounded to signal lunchtime. Stark thought fleetingly about food, but his gastric juices didn't react. All his physical being required at the moment was rest. But first, an emotional need had to be satisfied.

It would take time. The valley under Snowy Ridge was empty, with everybody crowded into the hotel to eat. If the absence of Angelo Spagnoli and Charmaine was noticed, it was not considered important enough for an investigation to be launched. The hotel and its adjacent building connected by the enclosed walkway across the ravine remained as quiet as the valley was empty.

He fell asleep.

It seemed as if he had merely blinked his eyes. At one moment he was peering through the telescopic sight, drawing a bead on the doorway of the hotel. The next, he started. The rifle lay in the snow and he was looking into his own armpit. But it was much longer than a momentary blink. The position of the sun marked it at something close to three hours. Lunch was long over and the valley was dotted with moving figures again, its peace disturbed by the distant sounds of laughter and shouted words.

Cursing himself, Stark snatched up the rifle and raked it to left and right, up and down. It took him ten minutes to locate the stocky, pot-bellied figure of Rick Essex. The top man in the Canadian arm of the company was in an appropriately high position. He stood on the platform at the highest point of the ski-jump. The telescopic sight zoomed him into close-up image. He was laughing at something Charlie Swenson had said to him. The younger man was preparing for a jump, wearing goggles, hard-hat, ski-suit and with his hands through the straps of sticks.

He moved forward to push his skis out over the lip of the platform. Essex placed a hand on his shoulder to give Swenson a shove off. Stark rested the barrel of the rifle across the tip of the sled runner. He steadied it, drew in a deep breath, held it – and squeezed the trigger.

The 7mm magnum shell penetrated the side of Essex's head and exploded into his brain. The impact should have knocked him backwards, but dying nerves closed his fingers into a claw to fasten on the material of Swenson's ski-suit. Swenson thought this was the expected push, and tipped forward to start the hurtling slide for the jump. The drag of Essex's dead weight toppled him. Both men went off the platform to smack into the hard-packed snow. The living became separated from the dead. But there was little difference in their rate of descent. Essex limply, and Swenson flailing skis and sticks, they crashed down the steep incline. When the tumbling, rolling forms reached the level-out at the lip of the jump take-off, they had too much forward momentum to stop. Both men crashed over the edge and plunged downwards. A zig-zagging, broken line of blood marked a trail down the run to show the course Essex had taken.

'This company's the same as any other,' Stark said. 'When a man's at the top there's no where else to go but down.'

He pushed himself to his feet and, once more, the excitement of the kill exploded a bolt of energy through him. A stronger one now, because he was physically more responsive to mental dictates after the eerie sleep. All over the valley the beautiful young girls and handsome young men had halted in their tracks. To stare towards the inert figures beneath the lip of the ski-jump, then to search for the source of the killing shot. The burst of noise from the sled's engine marked Stark's position and every eye swung towards the edge of the trees.

Stark, clearly visible against the white of the snow and green of the trees, raised the spiked wheels and shoved the sled into a downhill slide. The engine was superfluous, of course. Except that it gave every man and woman in the valley the opportunity to spot him before he opened fire. It was just an idea that appealed to him.

He snatched up the A-R 18 first, and sent a hail of deadly fire down the slope in short, raking bursts. Everyone was moving now – spurting for the hotel. But at least a dozen didn't make it as the heavy calibre shells ripped into them.

They pitched forward or toppled sideways, spreading crimson stains across the snow.

The sled zoomed down the slope, gaining speed with every foot it covered.

When the automatic rifle's magazine was empty, Stark snatched up the Savage. This was slower to exhaust, as he used the telescopic sight again, varying his targets between people on the ground and those, more helpless, descending in the chair lift. Bodies slumped to the snow. Others folded forward and hung from the high cable, dripping blood.

The sled hissed off the slope and slowed going across the level snow. Men and women on skis and on foot scattered out of its path.

The Savage clicked empty. Half the male and female whores were on the steps of the hotel, fighting and clawing each other to get into the cover of the building.

The sled stopped. At the side of the now empty ice rink, thirty yards from the steps. Stark went down on one knee, gathered up the automatic rifle and a fresh magazine and snapped them together. He stayed down to sight over the thousand yard range, his finger flicking the safety-catch to rapid-fire.

He squeezed the trigger.

A stream of orange tracer bullets lit a bright course down the slope. He was short of the target and snow spurted ten yards away from the stationery sled. He leaned back, elevating the barrel, and the long, slender, disjointed finger of bullets probed at the sled.

The explosive detonated. An orange ball bounced into the air and expanded. Blast ripped it into a million separate flames and these arced across the snow. Black smoke whirled. Fire rained down on the struggling throng. The plate glass wall shattered and flying glass became a new weapon of death. The pool water became tinted pink by blood billowing from ghastly wounds. Broken, burned and bleeding bodies were slumped in the snow outside and floated in the coloured water inside.

Stark straightened up, grabbing the Savage. He took a final look down at the carnage. Too many were left alive. More than half. Perhaps three-quarters. But there was nothing he could do about it now. At least he had got the top man and taken out more than a handful of lesser mortals. When it was a single individual against the might of the company there would always be more left alive than he could kill.

'So you can't win the game, mate,' he told himself as he whirled and started to run through the snow to where the Plymouth was hidden at the side of the road. 'But you can't say you don't get the odd bang out of it.'

A Selection of General Fiction from Sphere Books

A Selection of Sphere Westerns by Zane Grey